Consequences

By Amber Fawn

ISBN: 978-1-3999-7563-6

Content warning: This book contains content that may be troubling to some readers. Including, but not limited to, murder, abuse, sexual content, drug and alcohol use, trauma.

CHAPTER 1:

TROUBLE

Under the fading streetlights, my heart races as I join my cohorts, a tight-knit group of misfits with an obsession for trouble. With each stolen engine we rev, we defy the tedious routine-filled lives that attempt to suffocate us. Trouble is easy. Petty crimes have become second nature. Relay theft is as simple as tying a shoelace. Even so, the adrenaline rush is something I'll never get used to. The buzz. It consumes my mind entirely, dismantling any rational thoughts I may have left.

That pull of adrenaline has become too strong to resist. It's like primal instinct.

I'm fully aware that at almost 20 years old I should be spending my Tuesday very differently. At 3 a.m. sleeping would be the obvious alternative; playing a game or even going to a club if you're the more *'rebellious'* type. But that's too normal. Too stable. We were never given that opportunity.

Tonight's car is one of the better ones we've 'borrowed'. Starting the engine and hearing the growl of that exhaust is intoxicating; there's no sound quite like it. I press my foot on the clutch and rev the engine loud, just to add a little extra danger. Pulling off unnecessarily fast just so I can feel the car's power rush through my body. Rolling the windows down and blaring the music loud enough to feel the speakers pound is essential. Non Negotiable. I'm in control. That's where I like to be. Sienna touches my arm from behind and leans forward with a concerned look on her beautiful face.

"Is that a new tattoo?" She asks.

"Yeah, my mate did it for me at his house a few nights ago."

"You're gonna run out of space for them soon." I can't help but smirk at the adorable dose of genuine concern in her voice.

"Does that turn you on?" I ask, raising an eyebrow at her, forcing her to behave and sit back in her seat.

Such a pretty little thing.

"Marcus, look!" Skylar shouts.
I turn to my right, knowing exactly what I'm about to see. The others. Specifically Dean.

The pungent scent of marijuana punches its way through our windows and the thumps of their music match up almost perfectly to ours. Gorgeous. I look past Delilah who's sitting leisurely in the passenger seat, of course; their lovey-dovey relationship makes me sick. Dean is grinning assuredly from ear to ear, knowing full well he's about to speed past us. He puffs his joint before shouting over.

"In a bit, mate!" he laughs.
I've been challenged.

I put my foot down to the floor and hear the wheels squeak from under me. The wind whips us through the open windows. I catch glimpses of Dean smirking and Birdie waving smugly out of the back seat window as we alternate between first and second place. The road is ours. Traffic lights are nothing but an obstacle right now. I weave in front at the bend of the road. I know I'm pushing my luck, but the thrill has a hold of me. It has me hostage. Dean takes my risky move as a provocation. *What a surprise.* We reach the motorway, the unofficial-official final stretch. Almost instantly I hear a wheel spin from the side of me and I'm forced to swerve out of the way as Dean cuts me up, beeping the car horn to mock me as he knows his move gives me no choice but to slow down. He brakes slightly to allow me to catch up.

"Better luck next time, ay?" he gloats.

"Don't flatter yourself, you got lucky" I say, jokingly trying to protect my pride. We cruise for a while just taking in the moment. Letting it engulf us. Allowing it to teleport us back to when we were kids, just for a little while. I'm zoned out, in a world of my own. I'm happy. Through my daydream, I vaguely notice Dean dart off abruptly and Sienna leans through from the backseat to switch off the music.

"Uh Marcus, what are you waiting for exactly?" she says in a soft but panicked tone. I catch the flashing lights in the rearview mirror and sirens are suddenly flooding my ears. I'm jolted back into reality.

"Fucking drive!" Skylar yells. My foot hits the floor and we're all pushed back into our seats. The force of the acceleration is unsettling this time. We're in trouble.

"Call Dean, now." I instruct as I swerve bluntly onto the slip road. Residential areas are the best for a chase. They make it easier to veer out of sight. They're tight, cluttered.

"Yo" I hear from Skylar's muffled phone speaker.

"Where should I head?"

"Lose 'em and get to Orchid's, bro. We'll get the gate open."

"Sounds good."

The key to a police chase is to keep your cool. Think logically. Outsmart. With every turn I navigate, I'm planning the next five. My dad taught me how to drive; how to handle high speeds. He tells me I'm a natural-born driver. In fact, that's about the only nice thing he's ever told me. Getting caught isn't an option. Isn't something that even crosses my mind. I don't get caught. I figure everything out. The girls are alternating between gripping the grab handles and the back of the front seats. Albeit this is due to the abrupt turns, not fear. They know they're in safe hands.

I'm gaining ground now, naturally. They're struggling. I'm closer to the meeting point; a mere few minutes away under normal circumstances. Time to end the chase. I accelerate for the last time, pushing the car to its limit. This area is etched in my memory; I know every road, alley, and dead-end like the back of my hand. After a couple of ridiculously fast turns, I become very aware of the lack of flashing lights in my rearview mirror. The sirens are fading. I approach the gate. Open, as we agreed. I swerve into the dirt road and through the open gate; my wheels spinning out as I decrease my speed. Driving in, I pull far enough to vanish from view. Engine off. Silence. We instinctively lower our heads, a reflex more than a necessity, and listen to the coppers race past behind us. They've been outwitted.

Checkmate.

CHAPTER 2:

ORCHID'S

Without exception, the realisation of what had just transpired is always comical. I understand it shouldn't be, yet it always manages to elicit a chuckle. The novelty never wears off. Those brief moments of lifting our heads, sharing an exuberant glance, and truly comprehending that we've pulled it off once more. Turning to the front, I rub my hand on my forehead and I can feel my arrogant smirk forming. Skylar leans in from the back, checking my expression, and soon enough, she's giggling along with me. Both of us revelling in a conceited sense of relief. *Meanwhile, Sienna is*

likely a beautiful bundle of stress in the backseat.
Dean opens my door, laughing hysterically, with his joint still in hand. Admittedly, seeing him without one would be an odd sight. The smell of weed follows him. It lives on him. Sunken into his skin. It's one thing we have in common.

"You alright?" he asks, still lightly chuckling.

"Wonderful." I reply, somewhat sarcastically. Stepping out of the car and onto the pothole-ridden dirt path, Dean boisterously pats my shoulder, as if he were a proud father.

We stand together and look towards the building. It's a moment of perfect stillness, only broken by the sweet melody of birdsong just beginning. The sky is yet to start its transition from darkness to light. The doors stand sealed, the windows barricaded. Debris litters the car park, an unsettling testament to neglect. There's a faint 'Orchid's Children's Home' sign that somehow clings on, a ghostly reminder of the past. My heart faintly aches with memories from the years I spent inside. What was once a place I thought of as my home now stands empty and forgotten, like a lost soul longing to be remembered.

"It's been a while." Delilah says softly.

"Yeah," I mumble, nodding my head, as the echoes of laughter and conversation that once filled the rooms now fill only my head. Though in reality, they had been replaced with eerie silence.

"Let's go in!" Skylar suggests. I immediately look to Sienna, knowing she wouldn't be fond of the idea.

"I'm not sure about that." She responds, fishing for our agreement.

"Why not?" Birdie questions. "Scared there might be ghosts?"

Sienna lets out a nervous giggle.

"Come on, It'll be good." I reassure her.

I wrap my arm around her for comfort as we slowly head up to the entrance, gathering our varied thoughts. More and more memories rush back to me with every step I take and I feel my heart racing in anticipation. The car park where I first learnt to ride a bike. The front steps that I used to draw on with chalk. The now-boarded-up windows we would throw snowballs at in the winter. With one foot pressed firmly to the wall Dean begins to pull on one of the boards.

"Bro, gimme a hand." Together we manage to pry it off and get through to the smeared, dusty window beneath. I take a short peek in whilst disposing of the wooden board but the inside is nothing but darkness. Dean begins scanning the car park as the girls peer through the window with their phone flashlights. He sets his eyes on what he's looking for and walks assuredly towards it. After picking up a large brick, he turns around to face the window and whistles. The girls look over at him as he signals with his hand for them to move out of the way. After taking a second to perfect his aim, he proceeds to launch the brick cleanly through the window. Classic Dean, smooth as smooth could be.

"Easy peasy." Skylar says, practically leaping through the now shattered window. I'm often unsure if she contains even a single drop of fear in her body. Dean follows, climbing effortlessly inside and instinctively turning back around to lift Delilah through. I'm aware that she is petite, but with the way Dean lifts her, I can't help but imagine she is entirely weightless. Following it up with a swift smack to her behind once she had safely reached the floor. A connoisseur of charm. I move toward the jagged, broken window, navigating its edges cautiously as I make my way inside. The glass shatters underfoot, emitting a distinct crunch as I land in the pitch-black space. Without a moment's pause, I extend my hand, reaching out to assist the girls as they navigate their way through the same window.

Once we all are inside, I retrieve my phone and activate the flashlight, casting a beam into the darkness that surrounds us. With a deep breath, I steel myself, gazing ahead, a peculiar sensation settling within me. Standing in the building that had once been so familiar, but now feeling like an unwanted guest in my own home. *Well, I am trespassing after all.*

The living room. Our living room. If I can still call it that. The peeling walls and cracked ceilings remind me that it's no longer the place I knew. Feelings of nostalgia wash over me. Our dead silence is screaming in my ears. Ringing. Most of the furniture has been removed, except from the sofa we would squeeze onto for movie night, now tattered and worn. Dean picks up an old gaming controller from the floor and dusts it off. He vaguely scans his eyes past all of us, who are watching him attentively, and lets out a light smirk.

"Mad." he murmurs as he stares back at the controller, turning it around as if to analyse it. I can practically feel him replaying the memories in his mind. We continue walking through the rooms; our kitchen now entirely empty. Dust and cobwebs consume this place. I step into the bathroom and catch a glimpse of my face in the cracked mirror. I didn't think it would ever see this version of me. I had never imagined that this very mirror would get the opportunity to reflect my now adult self. *Trippy.* Exiting the bathroom, I instinctively pull the door closed behind me, though the reason remains elusive. Perhaps habit, or maybe a simple gesture of respect. With each step through I'm inspecting every wall, every floorboard, every item that remains. It's as if I'm strolling through a personal museum, surrounded by the exhibits of my own past.

The office. We were never allowed in here. Which ironically made it the most appealing room; despite the fact that, to my knowledge, the only thing living inside was paperwork. Boring adult paperwork and the suffocating aroma of coffee. Stepping inside now I feel like I'm breaking the law. *Yet again, that's probably because I am.* Entering the room I feel somewhat disappointed. As a kid, it appeared vast, holding an air of mystery and grandeur beyond comparison. In reality it's just an office. A dull, little office. I pull out the chair and take a seat, just because I can. Evidently the others feel the same way, as they take their places on the few other chairs, the desk and the floor.

"This office is shit." Birdie states. You can always rely on her for a profound summary.

"That's one way of putting it." I reply with a soft chuckle. Skylar slowly stands up off the desk and approaches a large filing cabinet. She tugs several times on the drawer but it doesn't budge. She sighs, a touch dramatic, then glances over at me, silently beckoning for assistance. I scratch my head and point my flashlight towards the hideous, dark-wood desk in front of me in search of a solution. A couple of pens, a stack of sticky notes, a broken lamp and '*aha!*'. A paperclip.

"Here." I say, throwing her my tiny discovered treasure.

"Perfect, thanks." She gets to work immediately and begins straightening out the paperclip, leaving the ends bent. It's as if the method is deeply ingrained in her mind. It must be. She inserts one curved end into the keyhole and begins to turn. Left. Right. Left. Right. Finding the correct unlock position. Click.

"Voilà!" She exclaims. Her fingers begin flicking through the contents and she tilts her head to briefly read the titles of each document. She lets out a small excited giggle and turns quickly to face us.

"All of our old files are in here!"

"No way." We seem to all respond in unison, our eyes widening. She nods her head happily.

"Who's up first then?" Dean asks, rolling a new joint.

"That would be…" With determination, she resumes sifting through the files, her head slightly tilted in concentration. This time, her search is meticulous, her eyes scanning each page with rigour. She pulls out the first file and walks back over to the table, placing it down firmly. Meeting my gaze, she pivots the paper to face me.

"Marcus Bear."

CHAPTER 3:
MARCUS BEAR

Everybody gathers at the speed of light around the desk, leaning in to get a glimpse of my file.

"Aww," The girls screech in time with one another. My baby photo staring up at us. My unkempt hair and red flushed cheeks. Those eyes, full of hope and curiosity. Not knowing what life was, or what it had just thrown at me. It's bittersweet. Reading a summary of my childhood, written by a social worker or volunteer who likely didn't truly know me. Somebody who condensed my early life into a single form before heading home to a family of their own. But the truth is they probably cared for me. Tried for me. Thought they were helping me. Thought they were stopping me from becoming exactly what I am today.

CHILD INFORMATION RECORD
GREAT BRITAIN

NAME: MARCUS BEAR

DATE OF BIRTH: 21/06/2004

DATE OF ARRIVAL: 02/12/2006

REASON FOR ADMITTANCE: UNSAFE HOME ENVIRONMENT

ANY FAMILY STILL IN CONTACT: NO

ELIGIBLE FOR FOSTER/ADOPTION PROGRAMMES: YES

PERSONAL NOTES:

Marcus arrived at orchids at the age of 2, after social workers were called to his home following reports of consistent drug use by his mother. They found his home environment to be unfit and unsafe. His mother did not fight for custody and voluntarily admitted him to Orchids childrens home and cut all contact from that point. His father could not be located at the time.

Marcus' biological father made contact with Orchids and gained full custody on 18/09/2018.

It goes without saying that I have always been aware of the fact I was abandoned by my mother. It was never a secret. Even so, there was just something very different about seeing it written on a piece of paper, in black and white. It's all right here, and it's all so hard to read. Looking back now from my newly-adult perspective, it's hard to not feel a sense of bitterness. The thought of ever walking away from that sweet child is alien to me. I sit here now as a young man who has just spent his night 'borrowing' cars, evading the police and breaking into a building and I can't help but wonder if things may have turned out differently for me, if my mother would have kept me. Maybe my life could've been better. Maybe I would've been a good person. But then again, maybe not. Maybe I would've ended up just like this anyway.

I love my dad. I know he loves me too. I'm thankful for him giving me a home. An actual home. But I can't forgive him. Never. Looking down at this piece of paper and seeing those dates. 2006. 2018. Where was he for all of those years? I've never gotten an answer. How can you wait that long? I feel like the other people in my life haven't really thought to question it. In fact, not a single person ever has, but me. It makes me feel like I'm crazy sometimes. *'Aren't you just so happy your dad finally found you?'* Over and over. How could it have taken that long to 'find' me? I stayed in a children's home just a few streets away from where he lived. It makes me wonder, how genuine was his search? Did he put in any real effort, or was he even searching at all?

"Wow, you were here for a long time." Delilah says, snapping me out of my resentful daydream. I scrunch my nose and push away the paper; pretending I'm not interested. In reality, I'm just trying to avoid any conversation about it.

It's a strange concept, isn't it? I spent my whole childhood in this place, with my friends. We lived it together. I knew nothing else but this place and them. The fabric of my existence woven alongside theirs. This was my home. My normal. They're my family. Yet, talking to each other about the very reasons we were there in the first place is pretty much considered a no-go.

"You alright?" Dean asks, gripping my shoulder, joint still in hand.

"Yeah, fine mate." I respond with a slight chuckle. Skylar's gaze shifts to me with a gentle, caring expression, holding it for a beat longer than comfortable, almost crossing into an intensity that breaks the moment. Eventually, she turns around and starts walking back towards the filing cabinet.

"Who's up next then?" She says smiling. She starts flicking through files once again but stops quickly. A smirk forming on her face. She prances back to the table and places the file down.

"Only the greatest, most beautiful, most perfect person in all of the world."

CHAPTER 4:
SKYLAR FARMER

The atmosphere whilst looking at Skylar's file is completely different. It's funny. The room feels lighter. We all let out a few chuckles whilst reading through, including her. The truth is Skylar never cared about being here. Never cared about hiding away from her life here, or why she came here in the first place. In fact, I'm not sure Skylar truly cares about anything. She's one of life's luckier people; not because she hasn't had any issues. Quite the opposite. She just has an incredible ability to take a problem, no matter how big, and simply flick it away like a bug. She does what she wants and says what she feels. Never seen her cry.

Never had her bad actions catch up to her, nor do they seem to affect her. A fearless, guiltless individual.

CHILD INFORMATION RECORD
GREAT BRITAIN

NAME: SKYLAR FARMER

DATE OF BIRTH: 03/03/2005

DATE OF ARRIVAL: 02/11/2017

REASON FOR ADMITTANCE: BAD BEHAVIOUR

ANY FAMILY STILL IN CONTACT: NO

ELIGIBLE FOR FOSTER/ADOPTION PROGRAMMES: YES

PERSONAL NOTES:

Skylar was admitted to Orchid's at the age of 12 due to years of uncontrollable bad behaviour. She was removed from her secondary school after just a few months for truancy and threatening another student. Her parents contacted police and had her removed permanently from her home when she had snuck out in the early hours of the morning to meet with older friends and engage in illegal activity.

Skylar was adopted on 19/01/2019 and is settling very well.

"How the actual fuck did you manage to get adopted so fast with a record like that?" Birdie says laughing and shaking her head.

"Not to mention the face practically screaming '*trouble*'." Sienna adds. Skylar rolls her eyes and laughs along with us. As I listen to the group joke about Skylar's file, I admire her carefree attitude. The world is like her playground and I envy that. As I alternate between reading and looking at her I can't help but think of her as somebody who has truly mastered the art of living. Seeing her as a different species to me altogether. It has to be innate. Why can't I embrace life with the same fearlessness and self-assurance that she exudes? What sets her apart from the rest of us? Can I learn something from her '*example*'? Do I want to? Maybe it isn't as easy as it seems, to not care. Maybe not caring is more work. More strain. Though if that's the case she certainly doesn't show it.

"The real question is who let me take any kind of picture with those earrings in and my roots not touched up?" Skylar says with a disgusted look on her face.

"That makeup though." Birdie adds, with an approving look. "You should definitely do a dark lip more often."

"Alright alright. Who's next?" Dean says, rubbing his forehead.

"Aww, are we boring you, Dean?" Skylar says while sarcastically pouting her lips.

"When are you not?"

"Touché." And just like that, Skylar snatches her file, deftly folds it to fit into her back pocket, and saunters back to the filing cabinet. Her smile lingers as she swiftly plucks the next file, stealing a glance for herself before returning to us. She climbs up to take a seat on top of the desk this time and crosses her legs. She winks playfully at Delilah before placing down her record.

CHAPTER 5:

DELILAH FRANKLIN

I don't even have to look, I can simply feel everyone smiling. Not that her file is anything to smile at; but because we're proud of her. Happy for her. A kind, loving soul. If any of us deserved a family it was her. If anybody deserved a happy ending after being here, it was her. I can still remember the day she came back to Orchid's, shy and reserved, but always with a gentle smile on her face. I knew immediately she was special. Always eager to help others, to lend a listening ear. She had become like a little sister to all of us over the years. She's the glue holding us together. I mean, she deserves a medal just for putting up with Dean's bullshit.

CHILD INFORMATION RECORD
GREAT BRITAIN

NAME: DELILAH FRANKLIN

DATE OF BIRTH: 20/03/2005

DATE OF ARRIVAL: 11/05/2006

REASON FOR ADMITTANCE:
VOLUNTARY ADMITTANCE

ANY FAMILY STILL IN CONTACT: NO

ELIGIBLE FOR FOSTER/ADOPTION
PROGRAMMES: YES

PERSONAL NOTES:

Delilah was brought to Orchids by her mother at the age of 1 after she found she wasn't capable of parenting Delilah due to her mental state following the death of Delilah's father. Her mother committed suicide just days after bringing Delilah into our care. She was adopted by her grandmother on 29/08/2006

Delilah was returned to Orchids on 07/03/2012 following the unfortunate death of her grandmother and has been entered into the adoption programme once again

Delilah was adopted on 24/06/2016

After reading, Delilah kisses her fingers and touches them to her anklet. The anklet her grandmother gave her. I don't think she'll ever take that off. I wish I had gotten a chance to meet her. I wish I could've thanked her for giving Delilah the early childhood she deserved. She allowed Delilah to grow into herself. To keep her warmth and her hope despite everything the world threw at her. Had she arrived at Orchid's earlier, I'm not sure she would be the Delilah we know now. It's as if her grandmother was a guiding light for her, and still is. She used to always talk about how strong she was. I mean, after losing her child and taking Delilah in herself; having to hide her grief for her sake, it's no wonder she passed on that resilience.

I observe Delilah, noticing the subtle rhythm of her deep breaths as emotions bubble beneath the surface. Her eyes glisten with tears as she takes one more deep breath. She looks up and notices me staring.

"I just miss her, you know?" She says quickly wiping her tears with her sleeve. I nod in comfort as Dean wraps his arm around her and kisses her head. I can almost feel the weight of their love for each other. Despite the fact that they couldn't be more opposite, it's hard not to feel a sense of awe at how much they've been through together and how deeply they still care for one another. So opposite that they're almost identical. That's what makes them work. Their differences are irrelevant. The experiences they faced together have bonded them for life. You can't get away from somebody after sharing this home with them. They'll always be in your mind. In your heart. We're a part of each other whether we like it or not. More than a family.

"Should we stop looking through these?" Skylar asks, concerned.

"No." Delilah replies, wiping tears that had fallen down to her chin. "I'm fine. It's actually been pretty nice having some time to reminisce."

"You sure, baby?" Dean asks. Delilah looks up to him and nods. Taking it as a cue, Skylar moves to fetch the next file, easily locating it and chuckling as she carries it to the desk. There's a collective understanding among us as she approaches; the identity of the file's subject is evident to everyone.

CHAPTER 6:
BIRDIE KING

There are many ways I can describe 'princess-Birdie'. Problematic, self-obsessed, high maintenance, sneaky, a diva. An instigator. The definition of manipulative. The list goes on. She definitely takes on the 'fiery red-head' stereotype to the highest degree. The last kind of person I would ever choose to be friends with. The odd one out. Flawed. But I love her of course.

As exhausting as she can be, she stuck by us all. She's honest, sometimes way too honest. Reliable. Safe. Strong. That's all that truly matters and I wouldn't have it any other way. She's an important piece in our puzzle and life wouldn't be the same without her. Though I can confidently say I fear for any man who ends up with her. *She'll eat them for breakfast.*

CHILD INFORMATION RECORD
GREAT BRITAIN

NAME: BIRDIE KING

DATE OF BIRTH: 13/12/2004

DATE OF ARRIVAL: 23/05/2008

REASON FOR ADMITTANCE: NEGLECT

ANY FAMILY STILL IN CONTACT: YES

ELIGIBLE FOR FOSTER/ADOPTION PROGRAMMES: NO

PERSONAL NOTES:

Birdie arrived here at Orchids at the age of 3 after being removed from her parents custody when she fell from a window in the property and neighbours had made a report of neglect. Social workers removed her from the home and her parents are currently fighting to regain custody of her.

Parents are in regular contact.

Birdie's parents regained full custody on 01/02/2017

Birdie's file is funny to all of us. Birdie is funny to all of us. Because the truth is she never should've been at Orchid's in the first place. She never fit in here. Her story was an unfortunate but fairly simple one. She comes from an amazing family. Well, a snobby family if we're being blunt, but a loving one nonetheless. She was a bratty child and she misbehaved. Her parents never abused her, never neglected her. The fall was nothing but an accident, but Birdie is a drama queen. Always has been. Unfortunately, so was her neighbour.

Her parents remained steadfast by her side, advocating for her relentlessly during her time here. It was evident to all of us that they would eventually gain custody. The odd one out. Her experience was nothing like the rest of us. Orchid's was more like a holiday home for her. Always going out for trips. Always being sent money and gifts. A pampered little princess.

I probably should be envious of her. She had everything I didn't. Money, family, security. But I'm not. Not at all. That life isn't for me. The standards. The pressure to be perfect all the time. The false smiles at all those black-tie-snob-conventions they call 'get-togethers'. Not to mention the uncomfortable clothing. I could never handle it. Maybe that makes her stronger than me. In all honesty, I feel for her. She lives in a whole different world, a comfortable but lonely one. It's like she's living in a cage wrapped in gold. I don't think she'll ever be able to reveal her true genuine self, if there is one. She fears disappointing people. Underachieving. To me that sounds like a nightmare. To constantly be on display as a perfect example of what somebody else thinks is ideal. Even here at Orchid's where the standards are significantly low, I struggled being myself. But Birdie, well, she's on a whole other level. It can be sad to watch. I mean it when I say she doesn't fit in with us, but I worry sometimes that she doesn't really fit in anywhere. She's just existing. Living a life that was never truly hers to live.

"What's so funny?" Birdie asks, with a playfully offended attitude. Nobody responds, there's no need to. Instead, we all exchange glances, silently acknowledging the irony. Here we are, all struggling to find our place in the world; committing petty crimes for fun, yet we find humour in the one who has her life the most together. I glance over to Birdie. She's still laughing, but something in her eyes tells me she isn't truly happy. I never believe she is. Maybe deep down she feels guilty. Or maybe I'm projecting my insecurities onto her. Who am I to judge? Maybe she's completely content being a pampered princess. All I know is that I wouldn't trade places with her for anything in the world. Sure, my life is filled with a lot of shit, but at least I have the freedom to make my own terrible decisions.

Skylar stands up and makes her way back to the filing cabinet.

"Let's move on, shall we?" She says, still giggling slightly. Her fingers begin rummaging once again and she swiftly grabs the next file to place on the desk. The mood dampens.

CHAPTER 7:
SIENNA SAUNDERS

Sienna and Birdie are polar opposites, with one exception. They don't fit in, but in very different ways. Sienna is dorky. Quiet. Anxious. Beautiful. Sweet. She was never made for this life. She sticks with us because we're all she knows, but she's too good for us. She struggles to keep up, knowing deep down this isn't what she wants. She loves us, sure, but we're holding her back. I know she wants more for herself, but she's never been able to break herself free from the safety net we've created. If she was honest, she'd rather be at home right now, reading a book. She'd wish for a drama-free life. A simple life. A life that isn't filled with people like us. A life with her true family, not crime, drugs and endless therapy sessions. Something quiet. Happy.

CHILD INFORMATION RECORD
GREAT BRITAIN

NAME: SIENNA SAUNDERS

DATE OF BIRTH: 14/03/2005

DATE OF ARRIVAL: 22/09/2010

REASON FOR ADMITTANCE:
EMERGENCY ADMITTANCE

ANY FAMILY STILL IN CONTACT: NO

ELIGIBLE FOR FOSTER/ADOPTION
PROGRAMMES: YES

PERSONAL NOTES:

Sienna was brought to Orchids at the age of 5 by police as an emergency admittance directly from her school after her parents were involved in a fatal car accident. She has found settling here a huge change and has recently been secluding herself more. She will be monitored closely and has been given extra counselling sessions regularly.

Sienna was adopted on 20/12/2015

'*Everything happens for a reason*'. Well, Sienna is the reason I know that's bullshit. What reason could there be for what happened? For what justified purpose does a child go through losing both of her parents at once? I can't even imagine the pain. Dragged away from a life of unconditional love and happiness and ending up with us. She deserved a life of success. She deserves normal teenage troubles. Maybe sneaking out a couple times or arguing with her parents about how messy her room is. Instead she's stuck with a bunch of reckless, selfish write-offs who think we're invincible.

I remember the time the others had pressured her to smoke weed with us. She coughed and gagged like she was about to throw up. I could've killed them that day for fucking with her innocence. *Only I get to do that.* Though I thought in some ways it would help her. In reality it just made her more paranoid and anxious. She hated feeling like she wasn't in control of herself. And yet, she stuck around. I can't help but feel responsible for that. Knowing I played a role in dragging her down this path with us. Sometimes I wonder what would happen if we just let her go. If we leave her behind. Would she finally get the peace she deserves? Maybe go off to university and find a normal group of friends. Or would she spiral out of control? It's a scary thought, but one I can't help thinking about. I just want to change things for her. I don't want to be the reason she's stuck in this life forever. Plus I'm secretly too selfish to let her leave.

"You've always been so beautiful." Delilah says, admiring Sienna. She scrunches her nose, rejecting the compliment.

"Thank you, but-"

"There's no '*but*'" I interrupt. Sienna looks at me almost as if she's confused. "You're beautiful, sweet." I continue. She briefly smiles at me before looking down and fidgeting nervously with her hands. I wish she were easier to read. I can't work her out, but I so desperately want to. I watch her gorgeous curls bounce around as she lifts her head back up to smile at me. I can tell that I make her nervous. She makes it obvious for me, maybe on purpose. I suppose that's a good thing, yet I can't seem to get through to her the way I want to. It's like every time I feel something may be developing between us she builds a wall around herself.

There's just something about her that draws me in. I can't help myself when it comes to her. Maybe it's that infectious smile. Or maybe it's the look she gives me when she thinks I'm not paying attention. Whatever it is, I want it. She's my sweet angel. I want to give her the life she deserves. *Of course*, the darker side of me wants to pin her down. Break her. To have my way with her. Wrap my hand around that pretty little neck. But it doesn't matter what I want, because every time I get closer, she pulls away. I can't force her to open up to me, because I know how much she's been through. I'm just waiting for the day that she'll let me in.

I suddenly realise through my daydream that the whole room is silent. I zone back in and see them all smirking at each other. Everybody can tell I'm flirting. I'm sure they always can, yet she's never directly addressed it. Never flirted back. Well, not vocally at least. Just with her body language, and her eyes. *Always her eyes*. Those beautiful golden eyes. Like pools of rich, inviting honey. Sometimes I'm sure they light up with a mysterious glint, as though she has secrets she's not ready to share. I feel like she's playing a very long game with me, and I can't help but play along. I'm like a moth to a flame. Sometimes I worry that it's all just wishful thinking. What *I* want. Maybe she just knows deep down that she's too good to be with somebody like me. If that's the case, then she's right.

"You two done staring at each other yet?" Dean asks, raising an eyebrow. I rub my hand on my head and laugh gently, now praying for the moment to pass by.

"Well then ..." Skylar says smugly, "moving on."

"Not much suspense for this one is there?" Dean says, leaning back into his chair. Skylar approaches the filing cabinet to grab the last file, flicking her fingers through once again. Searching, and searching. And searching. We all look at one another in confusion. She turns to us and frowns.

"Hm ... Dean's file isn't in here."

"It's probably too long to even fit in there." Delilah jokes. Dean looks angrily at her, in an obviously playful way, before letting out a smirk and gripping her thigh tightly. Skylar uses the paperclip once again to open up the other drawers. Regardless of how many times I watch her do this, I can't help but be impressed. Where did she even learn it from? Where did she learn half of the things she does?

I vaguely glance back at Sienna to find her staring at me, her doe eyes wide and hazy. I raise an eyebrow and she quickly turns away. *Very cute of her to think I wouldn't notice.* I scooch myself closer to her and whisper a husky warning in her ear.

"Keep looking at me like that and we're gonna have a problem, sweet." She tries her best to hide her tiny smirk before standing up and moving somewhere else.

Skylar suddenly stops searching before pulling out a folder and popping it open. She reads for a few seconds and bursts out laughing. I guess she found it. She walks towards the desk still laughing hysterically, struggling to get any words out.

"Well the good news is, I've found it. But the even better news is that it's in a folder titled *'For the young offenders unit'''* Everybody erupts into laughter, including Dean who is now covering his eyes. Of course Dean would have his own separate folder. Why would he not? It's Dean. He takes one more puff of his joint and leans forward, his hand not leaving Delilah's thigh.

"Here we go."

CHAPTER 8:
DEAN DOUGLAS

Dean Douglas. How do I even begin to describe Dean Douglas? I think 'an absolute fucking nightmare' would be a good start. He's a problem. A lost cause. The type of person who enters a room and indirectly demands your attention. Not in a good way, not at all. Rather in a way that would make the majority of people run a mile in the other direction. He's blunt, disrespectful and has a temper that could rival a volcano on the brink of eruption. I don't think there's a single person who has had the pleasure of being in his presence that he hasn't lashed out at. He's a dangerous person. He's constantly leaving a path of destruction behind him. He's beyond change. Beyond any help. Dean is Dean, and you either deal with it, or you leave.

CHILD INFORMATION RECORD
GREAT BRITAIN

NAME: DEAN DOUGLAS

DATE OF BIRTH: 01/12/2004

DATE OF ARRIVAL: 07/01/2017

REASON FOR ADMITTANCE: ABUSE, DANGEROUS BEHAVIOUR

ANY FAMILY STILL IN CONTACT: NO

ELIGIBLE FOR FOSTER/ADOPTION PROGRAMMES: YES

PERSONAL NOTES:

Dean arrived at Orchids at the age of 12 after his mother filed a police report against him following a physical altercation between him and his father. Dean is showing worrying signs of anger and general bad behaviour including physical altercations with other children, personal drug use (cannabis) and leaving the home without permission. Must be closely monitored by staff.

Dean was found by the police after stealing a member of staff's car for a joy ride whilst in possession of cannabis. Staff did not press charges but Dean was taken to spend a year in a young offenders unit on 08/03/2019

He's a force of nature and his behaviour is alarmingly unpredictable. Even his words carry a sharp edge, capable of cutting through the toughest of skin. I certainly don't like to be on his bad side and as hard as it can be to admit, I'm afraid of him. I suppose it doesn't help that he is definitely physically intimidating. Around 6'1 and broad. And yes, whilst he may be a few inches shorter than me and he's not particularly muscular; he's toned and he's incredibly strong. Far stronger than me and far stronger than most people he comes across. Trust me, I've seen it all with Dean. I've seen him fight, throw objects across the room, break tables, you name it. But that's not what scares me about him. I fear his mind.

I've seen him manipulate people and situations to get what he wants. He's charming when he wants to be, but that charm is always laced with danger. It's like you're walking on eggshells around him, never quite knowing when he's going to snap. One minute he'll be laughing and the next he's storming out of the room, slamming the door so hard the walls shake.

Despite this, he's a brother to me. I admire him, and for some reason, I seem to crave his approval. I've seen glimpses of vulnerability in him, rare moments when he's let his guard down. There's this sadness in his eyes sometimes, like he's carrying the weight of the world on his shoulders. I can tell he's battling a lot in his mind. It's like he's permanently exhausted. Constantly on the verge of explosion, and his unyielding rage is the only thing driving him. There are moments where I see an entirely different side to him. Like when he's with Delilah of course. He treats her with such a gentleness, as if she's made of glass. He's smooth and charming. Perfect to her, somehow. He's a complex person, with many layers; and he's my best friend. A huge part of who I am. It's a constant struggle. Having to constantly remind myself of the person I know he truly is underneath the mean facade. To care about him so deeply. The part of him that's redeemable. Struggling to find equilibrium between his virtues and flaws.

Seeing the image on his file is disturbing. He looks completely broken, and so extremely young. Thinking that this was the Dean I first met is alien to me. He looks so vulnerable now. So hurt. The giant bruise on his tiny face is harrowing; especially knowing the circumstance. Yet at the time I can remember thinking it made him look strong. Tough. Threatening. I can assure you that those tears welling up in his eyes were gone as fast as they arrived. He wouldn't let anybody see him cry. No way. He was playing the tough guy character right from the start. He had to. It's how he protects himself. The epitome of '*Hurt them before they can hurt me*'.

"Shit, that's a hefty bruise." Skylar states.

"Yeah, he fucked me up that's for sure." Dean begins to laugh, almost nervously. He's hurting, I know he is. I wish he would just say it. The room gets uncomfortably silent. We're all thinking the same thing. We can see he's in pain but saying the wrong thing can make him snap, and trust me, nobody wants that.

"That was fun." Delilah says smiling, likely desperate to break the silence and make sure Dean doesn't have too much time to think. Dean having time to think is a recipe for disaster. It's all for damage control. He presses a tender kiss onto Delilah's forehead, understanding her intentions, before sitting forward, his gaze fixed on the floor. The weighty silence settles in once more, and this time, I sense the responsibility to break it resting upon my shoulders.

"Maybe we should carry on looking around." Dean briskly stands up and nods his head in agreement.

"I don't wanna look at this shit anymore." He snaps, placing his hand on Delilah's back, leading her out of the room. I look at the others; they look back at me and our eyes do the speaking. We're aware of the need to maintain an upbeat atmosphere for the sake of Dean, at least for the remainder of the evening.

I let the girls leave the room first, not because I'm a gentleman, but because I want to soak in the room one last time. *The big, scary office full of mystery and secrets.* Yet as I stand, towering over the furniture that lives here, I let it sink in once more, that it's really nothing but an office. A boring, crappy little office. I'm putting my innocence into perspective. The big dreams I had. All of the insane ideas and plans. None of which came to fruition, clearly. I'm back here, in this now-abandoned children's home after stealing another car. Failing in every aspect of my life. A loser with no purpose. That isn't what my younger self would've wanted. Not for any of us. I take one last moment before ducking through the doorway and closing the door behind me. Glancing to my left, I notice the others making their way upstairs, prompting me to follow suit. Each step I take feels like a moment to absorb everything around me.

The barren walls, the peeling paint. The dust and debris scattered across the wooden floor. I remember the days when all you could hear was the echo of children's laughter through the walls and the pitter-patter of feet. Getting told off for trying to bring our bikes inside. And as we grew, the sounds of thumping music and doors slamming were the usual. But today, I hear nothing but a haunting silence and creaks of doors that I'm sure never creaked before.

CHAPTER 9:

UPSTAIRS

As we make our way upstairs I attempt to shake away these melancholy flashbacks and focus on the present. It doesn't work. 1, 2 ,3, 4, 5, 6, 7, 8, 9, 10, 11, 12, 13, 14. 14 steps. As a kid, I had a habit of counting each step as I ascended or descended the stairs. I'm not sure why. It's not as if I was expecting that number to somehow change. The girls are chatting away, in their own little world. It's as if they're oblivious to the fact that the ghosts of our past are lurking in every corner of this place. My mind is a blur as we move from room to room. The tiny upstairs bathroom with broken tiles and rusty pipes. The room that once belonged to the girl is now completely bare, devoid of any belongings. Nothing but moulded walls and torn-up floorboards. A completely smashed window with cold air pushing its way through. Though, it feels much clearer than I remember. Probably because it isn't covered in clutter. Or that my eyes and throat aren't burning from the fumes of hairspray and perfume, smacking me in the face. I always used to wonder what they'd talk about. In all honesty, I still do. Though it's unlikely I'd ever understand it anyway. Girl talk isn't exactly my specialty. If it was, Sienna would be mine already.

Only one room is left now. The bedroom I shared with Dean. The door, shut. Just how I had left it. Part of me doesn't want to open it. I'm not sure I can handle being hit with the memories. I left everything here. There wasn't a single thing I wanted to keep. When my Dad came to take me with him, that was the start of a new chapter for me. Or so I thought. New chapter, same shit. I turn the stupidly-loose knob and push the door open. Turning back to look at Dean as I make my way in. He shoots me a comforting glance and follows my lead.

Everything floods back and crashes into me like a wave. The room, the smell, the sounds. All of my stuff. My entire childhood exists inside of this room. I make my way over to the single bed that's pushed up against the wall. The chequered grey duvet I left is just lazily placed on top of the bare mattress. The wall, once adorned with my cherished bike posters, now stands bare, the torn remnants lying desolately on the bed. Dean's hand finds its way to my shoulder, offering a reassuring touch amid the melancholy scene.

"You good, bro?" He asks.

"It's a mess." I respond. This seems to be the only thought I can articulate. For some reason, it's making me angry. It feels like our space isn't being respected. Yes, I know it's not our space anymore and maybe I shouldn't care at all. But I do. Why? Nobody else seems to. I'm zoning into every single scuff on the walls. Every single broken piece of furniture. I make my way over to our wardrobe and open it, half-expecting to find my old clothes still hanging there. But it's empty, not a single piece of fabric left behind. I feel my blood boiling up inside and my breathing getting heavy. I turn to face Dean, who is still standing by my bed, a look of understanding in his eyes. He knows exactly what this room meant to me. To the both of us.

I look at the walls again and spot the old writing from when Dean and I had planned to escape. '*Escape*' as if this was some kind of a prison. We wanted to leave this place behind. To go as far away as possible. Somewhere. Now standing in this room, I realise how foolish we were. Just kids. Dreaming of a life we didn't understand and were so painfully far away from ever having. Confronting the reality of my situation and accepting the fact that my life didn't pan out the way I always wanted is a hard pill to swallow. I close my eyes and take a deep breath. It's time to leave.

"Let's go." I say, my voice cracking slightly. As everyone starts to exit, I follow suit, moving with the group. But a sudden pause halts my steps, my gaze drawn to the corner of the room behind the door. The slightly lifted floorboard. That's when I remember the things I had hidden. I immediately crouch to the ground and begin pulling up the floorboard. It's much easier to lift than I remember. I swallow as I feel the memories flooding out of this space on the floor. As I pull out the cardboard box from beneath my heart is racing and adrenaline is running through my body. It's been years since I've even thought about this box.

It's as if my younger self is reaching out to me, trying to remind me of the things I once held dear. Shoving them in my face. With shaky hands, I open the lid to reveal a pile of photographs, some trinkets and a few drawings. The pictures are blurry and worn but the meanings of them are still so fresh. Some of them are pictures I had taken on my old disposable camera, and others are pictures I had been given. I can feel everyone watching me closely as I flip through to the bottom of the pile.

A photo my mother had given the social workers when she passed me over. Of us. I had pretty much forgotten what she looked like by the time I was old enough to understand. This was the only reminder of her I ever had growing up. No matter how much I despise that woman, I didn't have the heart to throw it away. So I kept it, but I kept it at the bottom. Always at the bottom. That fucking photo. I wish she would've just kept that stupid fucking photo. But that would've been too selfless. She had to give me that one extra problem. One extra thing to deal with; to battle in my mind. The woman is cruel by nature.

She wanted me to know what she looks like. To never forget what she looks like. She wanted to leave me with a teaser of a mother I never got. But me? She couldn't care less. Never cared to see what I looked like as I grew. Never called to see if I was okay. Never contacted at all. Nothing.

As I sit on the floor, staring at the photograph of my mother and I, I feel a knot forming in my stomach and a lump in my throat. I begin seeing stars and the room starts spinning. It's as if all of the emotions I ever had towards her are coming back in full force. All at once. Cutting through me like knives. I quickly shove the photo back to the bottom of the pile and slam the lid shut.

My sweet Sienna crouches down next to me with her hand on my back. I look at her in the eyes as her face fills with concern.

"I'm here." She says, "Take a moment, please." She accepts the box from my grasp with a deliberate slowness, her eyes never leaving mine. I reach out, resting my hand on her knee, steadying my breath. With a firm press of my palms against my eyes, I attempt to stave off any impending tears. Seeing my mother's photo again after all of this time had hit me harder than I could've anticipated. It's like opening an old, deep wound that never healed.

She was a stranger to me, yet I longed for her to have been different. Waited up every single night just hoping she would walk through the door. Constantly living in denial. I had tried to rationalise that maybe she just couldn't take care of me. That maybe the story I was told was a lie and, in reality, I was taken away from my loving mother by some *evil* police officers. That she was fighting desperately every day to get me back. But if I was honest with myself, which I am now, deep down I knew she just didn't want me.

Summoning the strength, I rise to my feet, and Sienna stands beside me, her hand a steady presence on my back. Though the others cast their gaze in my direction, no words escape their lips. Dean's firm grip on my shoulder is accompanied by a silent inquiry in his eyes, asking how I'm holding up. I respond with a nod, signifying that I'm alright. He moves past me toward the spot of the missing floorboard, crouching down to retrieve something hidden within. Rising to his feet, he turns around, revealing a book in his hand.

CHAPTER 10:
THE BOOK

"What's this then?" He says smiling at me. "'*Defeating the Dragon*' Written and Illustrated by Marcus Bear, 04/02/2016." My cheeks flush with embarrassment as I try to snatch the book back. Dean, of course, doesn't let this happen.

"It's just a stupid storybook I wrote."

"Still writing stories at 12?" He laughs.

"11 actually."

"Oh my bad, that makes all the difference." We all laugh and he begins trying to remove the clasp. His face stiffens as he clearly struggles to do so.

"Struggling there, tough guy?" I say jokingly. He smirks and motions a '*shh*' to me with his finger. Despite his persistent efforts, the clasp refuses to yield, drawing out the amusement among us. Even Dean joins in the laughter, scratching his head in mild bewilderment. Altering his hand position, he makes another attempt, but the outcome remains unchanged; no luck.

"Let me try!" Skylar demands snatching the book. She studies the clasp for a moment, gently brushing her fingers across the carved surface. She starts pulling, her jaw clenched in frustration as she mutters something under her breath. Despite her efforts, it remains steadfast, refusing to budge.

"Come on then, Miss Lockpick." Dean teases.

"Here, I'll do it." Birdie snaps. Everybody takes turns trying to defeat the lock, but to no avail. Surely it can't be that stuck? My turn. I grab the book and turn it to examine the lock. It's a standard book lock, the kind that should open effortlessly. I glance at everyone with a puzzled and judgmental expression before attempting it myself. With one finger I pop open the lock and '*BOOM*'...

A sudden, powerful force escaping from the book, ricochetes off of every wall surrounding us in a frenzied dance. Not a loud noise, but rather a deep and resonant sound that made the entire building vibrate. As if a giant hammer had just struck the ground, sending a ripple through the air and pushing us backwards. It lasts maybe a few seconds yet it feels like an eternity. My ears begin to ring intensely, feeling as though they might burst. My eyes start to water and my heart is beating wildly, pounding through my chest. We frantically look at each other, every face covered in panic. Immediately we're drawn to the abrupt sounds of pouring, heavy rain outside. Nobody speaks. We all stand frozen, unable to comprehend what we've just experienced.

"What the fuck was that?" Birdie says, her voice trembling. We all exchange glances but don't have any words. No answer to her question; because none of us know the answer. Though all of us long for the answer. I glance down at the book in my hands as I'm shaking uncontrollably. A book can't do that, it's just not possible. I look back up at Dean who is staring at me intensely.

"It's just thunder, surely." He says, trying to convince himself.

"Bro, what kind of thunder does that?"

"You got a better explanation?" I look at the book once more and begin flicking the clasp open and closed with my finger before looking back at Dean, saying nothing, but my movements are speaking for me.

"*Ahh* okay, so we've found a magical fucking book? Is this really where we're going right now?" He's right, it's crazy to even think something like that, but what other explanation could there be? I shrug my shoulders and Dean rolls up another joint as his hands are shaking terribly.

"What do we do?" Sienna asks, looking up at me in fear. I look at her and shake my head. I don't know what to tell her. With a heavy heart, she lowers her head, and I instinctively pull her close, wrapping my arm around her, providing a tight embrace for comfort. Dean takes a long puff of his joint.

"Read it." He demands.

"I don't know if that's a good idea, man." He begins slowly walking towards me and laughing vaguely.

"So you're telling me, you think you're some kind of *chosen one* who has not only found a magical book, but written a magical book and you're not even gonna read it?" We stare at each other for a few intense seconds.

"He's right Marcus, we have to read it." Skylar interjects. "What if there's something important in there?"

"There won't be, Sky, it's a shitty little fantasy storybook I wrote as a kid. Dean was right, it had to be thunder." The room fills with an awkward, lingering tension as I wait for somebody else to move on the conversation. I turn my focus to the rain outside; pounding down in a heavy rhythm onto the roof. Creating a background noise that is strangely soothing to me. Like a lullaby, calming my racing heart and anxious thoughts.

"Maybe we should get going." Delilah suggests.

"I agree." Dean responds, taking another drag. He briskly grabs Delilah and leads her out of the room, the rest of us following closely behind. As we make our way back to the broken window we climbed in through, I'm not taking in the building anymore. Not thinking about the memories I made here. I'm thinking about the book in my hand. The bang. The sudden storm. None of it makes sense.

We reach the smashed window and all I can hear is the relentless downpouring of rain. I pull up the hood of my jacket and climb my way out, the shards of glass cracking underneath my feet. We all run back to the cars, more than ready to call it a night. As the car doors shut, the silence is definitely noticeable. We all sit for a moment, exhausted, soaking up our thoughts.

"Marcus, are you okay?" Sienna asks.

"Yeah, sweet." I shoot her a smile through the rearview mirror. "I'm all good." She smiles back briefly and turns to look out the window, mesmerised by the pouring rain. Dean beeps a few times from the other car, before driving off recklessly. I turn on the car, 5:23a.m.

As I drive slowly, my mind is full. So many thoughts are racing through my head that I'm not thinking a single thing. It's all a blur. My head is thumping and my eyes are strained. The rain continues to pour down heavily, creating a white noise that echoes through the empty streets. I pull up to Skylar's house, my eyes barely staying open.

"See ya!" She shouts, smiling, as she gets out of the car, slamming the door behind her. Somehow still full of energy. *That girl can't be human.* I watch and wait for her to get inside safely. Well, *Safely* for Skylar, meaning I watch her climb onto the top of her porch and pull herself up through the top floor window. She waves enthusiastically at me and I nod back before turning to Sienna. Curled up on the back seat, fast asleep, using the seatbelt as a pillow. Suddenly my mind isn't so busy. All I can think about is how beautiful she is. How angelic. My sweet girl. I start up the car again, whilst smiling ear to ear, and drive it back to where we had taken it from. As I step out, grabbing the book from my lap and tucking it into the top of my joggers, I'm making sure to be as discreet as possible; trying not to make a single sound. I open the door to the back seat and give Sienna a gentle shake to wake her.

"Hey," I whisper. She stirs and rubs her eyes in the most adorable way possible before looking up at me. "You wanna just stay with me tonight?" She nods her head and smiles, shutting her eyes once again. I unbuckle her seatbelt and carefully lift her out of the car, shutting the door slowly with my elbow. As I take the short walk back to my house with Sienna in my arms, I'm at peace for the first time in a while. The only sound that fills the air is the soft chirping of birds. These moments, with just the two of us, hold a special place in my heart, even when not a single word passes between us. I feel grateful for the trust she puts in me; at this moment, holding her in my arms she's the only thing I care about. Protecting her. I'd kill for her safety.

I want to understand her. I want to know what to say to her, what she wants. Whatever it is, I'll do it. I want to be more than a couple of friends who flirt and that's it. I want us to do more than just 'like' each other.

That is, if she even likes me.

As I navigate the dark and quiet streets, all I can detect is her head resting on my chest, rising and falling with my breaths. Feeling her warmth seeping into my skin, I realise just how much I crave her affection. I want so desperately to kiss her, but I don't want to ruin any moment. I don't want to risk our friendship. While a friendship may not be exactly what I want, I'd take that any day over not having her at all. As I reach my front door, With one hand, I clutch my keys tightly, while the other remains a steady support around her. I unlock the door and lead us inside, the comforting warmth of home wrapping around us. Taking deliberate steps, I guide us up the stairs and into my bedroom, ensuring a gentle closure of the door behind us. I carefully settle her onto my bed, tucking the duvet cover snugly around her for comfort. I take a deep breath before taking a risk and gently pressing my lips against her forehead. She stirs a little before settling back into her slumber, the light from my desk lamp softly glowing on her skin. I begin taking off my shirt when I'm abruptly snapped out of my current paradise. The book.

CHAPTER 11:

'READ IT'

I hold the book in my hands and stare at it. Flicking the clasp and tutting nervously. Dean's instruction is repeating and repeating in my mind on an endless loop. 'Read it.'. It's pretty pathetic. Incomprehensible. Am I scared? Scared of a book I wrote myself? But it isn't just a book anymore, is it? It's a book that seems to have caused a fucking explosion and sudden storm. Am I losing my mind? I shake my head, trying to clear it and throw the book onto my desk. I need to sleep. To make the most of this moment with Sienna. But as I slip into the bed beside her and try to settle, my mind can't help but wander back to the book. It's sitting there smugly on my desk, taunting me. Impossibly, I can feel its presence in the room with us. It's like there's a weight in the air.

I try to push the thoughts away, instead focusing on Sienna's peaceful breathing and the warmth of her body next to mine. But it's no use. It's calling me. I can't just ignore it, can I? What if I'm not going crazy? There could be something important inside. What's the worst thing that could happen? I sit up in the bed and crack my neck, my mind made up. I'm procrastinating and I can't ignore it any longer. I climb back over Sienna and take a seat at my desk, glancing over at her to make sure she's still asleep before I open it. I hold my breath while opening to the first page, in preparation for another 'bang'. It's fine. No noise, no rain. Nothing at all. I take a breath of relief before my attention is brought to my childish drawings and terrible, sloppy handwriting. My skills were definitely not at the right level for my age. But is that surprising?

'The animals were asleep peacefully in the village, when suddenly they were awoken by the sounds of rain and thunder crashing above the houses and a loud ROAR in the distance. They all emerged from

their homes, and to their horror, they saw the very scary 'Derpy Dragon' rapidly approaching. Panic set in as they realised that their village was in grave danger.

'Baker kitty' immediately got to work, using her magic to whip up medicine potions and remedies to give the animals strength in battle. 'Sakura fox' scrambled desperately to protect the nearby flowers, while the army worked feverishly to fortify the village defences. But then, disaster struck, 'Shy spider' stumbled and fell, injuring one of her many legs. With one of the animals vulnerable, the animals had to move even faster to prepare. Time was running out.

At last, the Derpy dragon arrived, accompanied by his loyal sidekick who is 'definitely a Froggy'. The chaotic battle began and the village was soon awash with flames as the dragon breathed fire on the homes and shops. Despite their fear, the animals fought back valiantly, determined to defend their beloved home. All of a sudden, the dragon began losing energy, and fell to the ground, dead.

King 'Mint choc chipper' and Queen 'Milk 'n' cookies, deer?', who had been watching from the safety of their castle, waited for the dragon to die before emerging from the castle to inspect the damage brought by the dragon. Together, they closed the gates once again to protect their village.'

After reading I pause, almost expecting something crazy to happen. Maybe an explosion? A bang? Some kind of surreal beam of light like they have in the movies? Nothing. Just my bedroom. It's simply a tale straight out of a storybook—a mere thunderstorm. Why did I even entertain the thought of it being something more? Almost amusingly anticlimactic. With a quiet chuckle, I close the book, letting go of any lingering expectations. I try to seal the clasp which, for some reason, no longer closes fully and turn off the lamp. Once my eyes begin to adjust to the darkness, I make my way back into bed. As I lay down next to Sienna, she stirs again and shifts slightly closer to me. Taking another risk, I wrap my arm around her, pulling her close to my chest; the soft sounds of her breathing mixed with the chirping of birds outside lulling me to sleep.

Waking up a few hours later, Sienna's head still resting on my chest, everything feels right. I feel so weightless. So content. I trace my fingers over her cheek and make my way down to her neck, memorising every curve. I pull away from her gently, trying not to disturb her sleep, and grab my phone to check the time. 10:14. I get out of the bed quietly and decide to make breakfast for us.

As I brush my teeth and make my way to the kitchen the only thing on my mind is Sienna. My sweet. She's all I want. She's the only thing holding me together. The only thing in my life that makes me want to be a somewhat-good person. I stand still and glance around the kitchen, trying to decide what to make. Bacon sandwich? Pancakes? Too simple. I need her to know that I'm a good cook. Not that she would even care. She's too nice. A full English. That's it. I open the fridge and take out some eggs, bacon, sausages, baked beans and mushrooms and start cooking. The smell of sizzling bacon fills the room and I can just feel myself smiling. It's the perfect morning.

Taking a sip of my tea, I hear her faint little footsteps behind me. My heart is pounding with excitement and the butterflies in my stomach begin to race. I fix my hair and turn around to see her standing in the doorway wearing one of my hoodies and rubbing her eyes. It's an adorable sight which forces me to try and conceal my smile. I know I have to play it cool, but fuck, it's pretty much impossible when she looks like that.

"Good morning, sweet."

"Good morning." She replies with a smile, looking around at all the food I'm serving up. I nod subtly, feeling very proud of myself. I know I'm impressing her.

"I hope you're in the mood for a full English breakfast, *Marcus Bear style*." I say with a smirk as I set down her plate. She laughs and takes a seat at the table, pouring herself a glass of orange juice.

"You're good to me." she says taking a bite of bacon.

"And you're mean to me. In fact I'm the only person you're ever mean to," I pause, "and that really turns me on." She rolls her eyes and pouts, trying to conceal her smile. I can hardly focus on eating and can't stop myself from staring at her; the sunlight pouring through the window and bouncing off of her skin.

"You got plans today?" I ask.

"College is supposed to be today's plan." I check the time on my phone and smirk before flipping it to show her. 11:37.

"*Shit*." I say sarcastically. "Too late for that now I guess."

"What did you have in mind?" I shrug nonchalantly, trying to come up with an idea on the spot.

"Wanna go for a ride?"

"No. Not the bike."

"What's wrong with the bike, sweet?"

"I hate the bike."

"You don't mean that."

"I absolutely mean that." We both laugh and look at each other for a few seconds before I stand up and grab the bike key, tossing it in my hand.

"I'm serious, Marcus."

"So am I, *Sienna*," I raise my eyebrows and wait for her to change her mind.

"Fine, but no speeding."

"Okay, no speeding." I promise as I reach out my pinky finger. She stands up slowly, rolling her eyes and locks her pinky into mine.

"Maybe a little speeding." I tease as she walks towards the front door.

CHAPTER 12:

LEAVE THE CITY

We make our way outside and I can feel the cool breeze on my skin. The sun is shining, but what's funny is that if Sienna wasn't with me I probably wouldn't realise it. I'd be cooped up in my room with the curtains shut, smoking weed and wasting yet another day of my life. I grab my helmet and toss it to Sienna before hopping on the bike. I start the engine and rev it a few times before motioning for her to climb on. She does so reluctantly, wrapping her arms tight around my waist as I slowly begin to push off. The feeling of her heartbeat through my back is indescribable, like she's a part of me. I take things easy at first, not wanting to freak her out too much, but as we hit the open road I can't resist the urge to speed. I glance back at her briefly and she seems nervous. But excited at the same time.

We ride for hours through winding roads; the sun shining down on us. I can feel her grip tightening every time I pick up speed, and it's almost reassuring to feel her trust in me. Eventually, we start to pass by fields and farms and I can see cows and sheep in the near distance. The air begins to smell like freshly cut grass and wildflowers, which makes a refreshing change from the constant scents of petrol and cigarettes back at home. Places like this make me feel like I'm taking my life for granted. Like I'm missing out. I'd do anything to live in a place like this. I take a deep breath and let out a laugh, glancing back at Sienna. We eventually reach a small clearing near a river and I decide to park the bike, both of us climb off and take a moment to breathe in the clean air. I stroll over and take a seat on the grassy bank, briefly dipping my fingers in the water.

The water feels stimulating and cool against the skin of my fingertips and I watch as it ripples and fades away. Sienna soon joins, sitting down beside me and staring out into the fields. We sit in a comfortable silence for a while. Peace. Quiet. I look around and take in all the vibrant colours and the gentle sway of the tall grass in the breeze. Vibrancy is rare for me. More often than not, everything seems grey. Desaturated. I riskily place my hand on Sienna's leg before removing it quickly and deciding to roll up a joint; lying back to take a drag. Looking up at the sky I feel like the kid I never got to be. Safe and secure.

"Isn't this just the ideal place to be?" I say, closing my eyes. "I hope we can leave that fucking city one day."

"I agree," She replies lying back with me. "But it has some positives."

"Such as?" She pauses in thought for a moment.

"The lights at night time are pretty beautiful."

"*Ah yes,* the lights. They definitely take my mind away from the never-ending traffic, crippling pollution and high crime rates."

"You say that as if you aren't constantly adding to those high crime rates." We both laugh and look into each other's eyes.

"How do you do it?" I ask.

"Do what?"

"Find the good in everything." She shrugs and looks back up to the sky.

"Everything bad has something good. You just have to look for it." I take a moment to think about her answer; the sound of the river flowing in the background.

"A rabbit!" She shouts, practically leaping to her feet. I sit up slowly resting my arms up on my knees and take another puff. Across the river, a small brown rabbit sits, quietly observing from the other side.

"I wanna cuddle it."

"You can't cuddle a wild rabbit, beautiful." Before I can even fully finish my sentence she has taken off her shoes and socks and started rolling up her very baggy jeans.

"What are you doing?" I laugh. She doesn't respond as her mind is entirely fixated on the rabbit. Finding a shallow part of the river broken by rocks, she starts stepping across with her hands flicked upward, like a little princess. With every step, the rabbit is becoming more aware of her presence and beginning to distance itself.

"It's okay, bunny." She says, softly. Her face fills with determination and she begins to rush. As she takes her next step I notice her foot slipping, almost in slow motion, and she falls onto the rocky edge of the river.

"Sienna!" I shout, knowing it's impossible to catch her. I quickly throw my blunt and run into the river; the water almost reaching up to my knees. I quickly lift her up and carry her out of the water and onto the soft, swaying grass.

"Are you okay?" I ask.

"My leg hurts pretty bad." I look down at her leg and see a small amount of blood sitting on top of a significantly large scrape. I swiftly make my way to my bike and start searching through the rear compartment to locate my first aid kit. As I open the kit and take out some antiseptic spray and a bandage, I notice Sienna staring at me. Her eyes filled with amusement, as if she's discovered a whole new part of me. She looks down, but I can see a smile tugging the corners of her mouth. I gently crouch down beside her and spray her wound. She winces briefly, clutching my hand tight.

"Sorry, this might sting a bit."

"It's okay. I'm sorry I ruined the peaceful moment."

"You didn't ruin anything, sweet" I reassure, bandaging up her leg. "Just a little mishap, that's all." She looks up at me and suddenly our eye contact is very intense. I feel my heart pounding and there's a silence between us, as if the world around us has frozen in time. I'm entirely captivated by her. Her eyes, the way she looks at me, her hair, her lips, her skin. That tiny hand gripping mine. My mind is racing with a million thoughts at once, each telling me to stop being a coward; to tell her how I feel.

"I'm in love with you." I confess. She looks shocked as her mouth opens slightly and her eyebrows scrunch, but I can't stop there. "There's nobody like you, Sienna. Nobody. And I'm sorry if this is a lot to take in but I just can't pretend anymore."

"Marcus," she says, shaking her head.

"Look, I know you're above me. *Believe me,* I fucking know that. I'm not the best man there is, far from it, but I also know that nobody else will love you the way I do." She doesn't respond, or move, but her eyes begin to widen. I start leaning in and she does the same. Her beautiful little face, flushed with nerves.

"We should go." She says abruptly. *What?* I look down and try to register what just happened, before pulling away and clenching my jaw in embarrassment. Staring into the abyss, I slowly lift her to her feet, cherishing the touch of her hand, and begin methodically packing away my first aid kit. The action is mechanical, a physical distraction. I can see her from the corner of my eye, standing awkwardly beside the bike as I walk to grab our helmets.

"Marcus I'm sorry, it's not you. I just-"

"It's cool." I say, cutting her off and passing her the helmet, our hands brushing briefly as she takes it. We both slip them on and mount the bike, the engine roaring to life.

"Ready?" I ask, looking back. She nods and wraps her arms around me, squeezing me tight for some reason. Everything she does is confusing. This can't be in my imagination. Is she scared? Playing with me?

As we drive back towards home, I can feel a tension we've never had before. I've ruined everything. My heart begins to sink lower and lower with every passing moment. I should've kept my mouth shut. But I was so close. I notice her grip loosen, both physically and emotionally and I'm kicking myself. All I can hear is the engine. Each time we stop I can feel her eyes on me, but I don't want to look back. I don't want to see her face, flushed with disappointment or confusion. I don't want to explain myself. As we finally pull up to her house, I park the bike and take my helmet off, turning to face her. She's avoiding eye contact but is forced to look at me while returning the helmet. She smiles at me briefly.

"Thanks for today, I had fun." She says softly.

"Of course, sweet."

"I'll uh… text you later?"

"Yeah, cool." We both force a smile but I know I can't let her go like this. She begins walking away but I impulsively grab her hand and pull her to face me. Those perfect eyes staring right into mine.

"I didn't mean to make things awkward."

"It isn't awkward." She lies.

"Oh *really*? Because it feels pretty fucking awkward to me."

"I just need time to think, Marcus." She turns and walks away, not looking back. I wait for her to get inside and I snappily put my helmet back on. As I ride home, way faster than I should, I can't help but feel like everything is falling apart. My heart aches as I go over every word I said to her, over and over. I can't lose her.

Before I walk back into the house I check my phone, hoping she'd messaged me. But there's nothing. No message. Nothing.

"You've fucked it." I murmur to myself. Home shit home.

CHAPTER 13:
FAMILY DYNAMICS

Walking back through the door feels so wrong. I feel entirely helpless. I should be doing something to fix this. Tossing my keys onto the side table, I walk through to the kitchen and grab myself a beer from the fridge.

"There 'e is!" My dad shouts, stumbling into the kitchen. His 'demon dog' following closely behind. The last person I want to see right now. "Y'alright mate?"

"Yeah dad, I'm good."

"Where ya been?"

"I just went for a ride."

"On your own?" I take a deep breath as I open my beer and begin drinking, knowing this conversation is about to go south.

"Nah, with Sienna."

"Ahh, Sienna ay?"

"Yup."

"She ya girlfriend yet?"

"No, she's not." He begins laughing obnoxiously and raging anger starts to build up inside of me. I take another swig of beer and look him dead in the eye; as usual he doesn't take my hints to shut up.

"*Cor*, you move a bit slow don't ya mate?" He continues to laugh and hits my shoulder. My mind is thrown back to the files we had found.

"That's ironic." I mumble under my breath. His laughs quickly softens.

"What was that?"

"I said, that's ironic." He has the nerve to look at me with confusion.

"What you tryna say?"

"Well, I don't know about you but I'd say that taking over 10 years to *find* me was pretty fucking slow."

"Excuse me?"

"You heard me." I start, "I stayed 15 minutes down the road in a children's shelter and you actually expect me to believe you were making any fucking effort to find me? You weren't doing shit."

"You have no idea what I was doing out there, boy. Watch your fucking mouth."

"Or what?" I walk up to him and lock my eyes to his. I'm seeing red.

"I'm your father."

"So you keep reminding me. If only you'd bothered to show up when I *actually* fucking needed you. I brought myself up. I had to take care of myself while you were off doing your own thing. You're a complete joke." He takes a step closer to me, his breath smelling like whiskey and cigarettes.

"Say one more word boy, I dare ya."

"I'm not a boy. I'm a grown man now. You missed that part, remember?"

Suddenly, he lunges at me with a closed fist and gives me no time to react before I feel the impact of his hand against my jaw. The pain is sharp and intense, causing me to lose balance briefly and stumble backwards. The room falls silent as we both stare each other down. His eyes are filled with a burning rage and I can feel my heart rate increase rapidly. I catch a glimpse of the vein pulsing in his forehead. The anger and resentment between us is palpable, vibrating in the air like an electric current. The room feels so much smaller now and I can taste the copper of blood in my mouth. I want to kill him, but instead I freeze entirely. Without saying a word he turns and begins walking to the front door.

"Scumbag." I say, shaking my head.

"You better be gone by the time I get back." he responds, slamming the door so hard I can feel the house shake.

I stand there, alone in the kitchen, trying to process what just happened. Anger, sorrow, and frustration interlace within the tumult of my thoughts. I hear the sound of my dad's car engine roaring outside as he speeds away, leaving me behind once again. *Deja vu.* Seeking solace, I take another sip of beer, endeavouring to pacify my frayed nerves, and walk over to the sink to splash my face with water. The chill of the cold water is relieving against my burning skin. I grab my phone from my pocket and text Skylar, asking if I can crash at her house. Her family treats me like I'm one of them. Sometimes I wish I was. Her home has become a welcoming escape zone for me, like an oasis in the chaos of my life.

I head upstairs and start packing a bag. It's not the first time I've had to do this, but I have a different feeling now, *and a much bigger bag.* There's no going back this time. As I'm about to leave the room a peculiar sensation creeps in; a nagging feeling of forgetting something vital. Pausing, I pivot to survey the room, and there it is staring me in the face. The book. I couldn't care less about that book. I had forgotten it even existed for years whilst it was left to rot under a floorboard. But I do care, subconsciously. I quickly grab it and stuff it into my bag before heading out.

I hop on my bike and ride towards Skylar's house, my mind still reeling. The wind rushes through my hair, momentarily distracting me from the swirling thoughts. I try so desperately to focus on the road ahead but everything is passing me in a blur. I'm riding recklessly, but this time, it's not deliberate. The blaring of multiple car horns pierces the air, more than usual, directed at me, but I'm at a loss about what I'm doing wrong.

Miraculously, I arrive at Skylar's house, despite navigating the route without a single conscious thought. Disembarking from my bike, a heavy weariness settles in. I can tell I'm both emotionally and physically drained. I crack my neck in an attempt to alleviate some tension before advancing toward the door. The faint, comforting sounds of laughter and chatter emanate from the living room window.

I take a deep breath and knock on the door, setting aside my unease. Skylar opens the door almost instantly, with a concerned look on her face.

"You okay?" She asks.

"Yeah, just another argument."

"Marcus, your face-"

"I know. Don't worry about it."

She moves to the side, staring in shock at my jaw, it must be bad. I step inside, gently slipping off my shoes and leaving my bag on the stairs. Skylar guides me into the living room, where her parents are cosily seated, engrossed in a film.

"Oh my goodness!" Her mum shrieks, jumping off of the sofa. "Darling what happened?" I shrug it off and reach out for a hug instead.

"Was it your old man?" Her dad asks, standing with his arms crossed. I nod to him.

"Yeah, things just got heated. I'm fine though." Her parents exchange a worrying glance before her dad takes a breath and speaks again.

"Well, you stay here as long as you need to, okay? I'll set up the spare room for you in a bit."

He says, placing a comforting hand on my shoulder. I feel a lump forming in my throat and I'm forced to swallow my emotions. At this moment I'm wishing for a different life. For a life with parents like hers; ones who actually care about me instead of seeing me as a burden, punching bag or inconvenience. It's all so foreign to me. Did I not deserve it? My mind wanders to memories I've been suppressing; memories of loneliness and feeling unwanted. I feel an overpowering wash of sadness for my younger self. For that little boy who deserved better. Skylar's mum thankfully saves me from my own thoughts and returns me to reality by gesturing me out of the room.

"Come on Darling, let's get you sorted out."

I follow her into the kitchen, taking a seat at the large dining table while she rummages through the drawers. Skylar walks in shortly after, grabbing herself a small stack of biscuits before taking a seat next to me. I take the moment to collect myself and relax; the warmth of Skylar's home soothing me. Her mum grabs some antiseptic cream from a first aid kit and grabs a seat opposite me. She gingerly begins to apply the cream to my wound, leaving me with a sharp, stinging sensation which quickly cools and spreads outwards across my hot and swollen jaw. The sensation is almost refreshing as I begin to feel it disinfecting. The scents of the cream and air freshener mixed with the sound of Skylar's brothers laughing upstairs is creating a heartwarming atmosphere that I long for. I close my eyes and take a long breath, a slight smile forming on my face. Feeling a hand rest on top of mine, I open my eyes to see Skylar's mum smiling at me.

"Feeling better?"

"Yes, Thank you."

"No need to thank me, Darling. We just want you to be alright."

"Do you wanna talk about it?" Skylar asks, taking a bite of her final biscuit. I look at her and shake my head briefly.

"It's just the usual shit."

"I know just the thing you need." Her mum says suddenly, standing up and walking to the bottom of the stairs. "Boys! Come down! Game night!"

In no time, Skylar's younger brother bounds down the stairs as her mum quickly scurries off to grab the games.

"Marcus!" He exclaims, running to me for a bear hug. Her older brother following, slightly less enthusiastically, behind and greeting me with a simple nod of the head.

"Y'alright bro?"

"Yeah, all good."

"You been in a fight?" he asks.

"Nah, it's nothing man." We spend the rest of the night playing through all of the board games they have and eating snacks, the tension from my day dissipating slowly. The sounds of laughter and the joy of both winning and losing fills the room and I feel like a part of the family once again. My mind letting go of the turmoil and becoming entirely occupied by the positive atmosphere as my jaw begins to ache from the constant laughter. The warmth of the room and the softness of the sofa against my back making me feel safe. For a moment, my thoughts briefly turn to Sienna, and I feel a pang in my chest. I take my phone out of my pocket and check for messages, but still nothing. I toss my phone onto the carpet and allow myself to get lost in the moment once again; to be present.

As the night wears on and the games come to an end, Skylar's dad begins setting up a bed for me in the guest room.

"There you go, mate. I'll get some more pillows down for you tomorrow when I have a moment."

"This is more than fine for me, thank you again."

"No need to thank me. Get some rest."

"Will do." He shuts the door as he leaves the room and I immediately fall backwards onto the bed, staring up to the ceiling and listening to the sounds of the house settling. I hear some footsteps coming up the hallway and a faint knock on the door.

"It's me, the Monopoly champion." Skylar says through the door.

"You can come in." I laugh. The door opens and Skylar bounces in, sucking on a lollipop and flopping down onto the make-shift sofa bed.

"So, talk to me, loser. What's going on with you?" I laugh at the simplicity of her question.

"How much time have you got?"

"Marcus, I don't sleep until at least 3am and It's currently only 10. I have all the time in the world."

"Fair. Well I'll cut it as short as I can." I let out a loud breath before starting. "So, Sienna stayed at mine last night-"

"In your bed?" She interrupts, winking at me.

"Yes Skylar, in my bed."

"Nice." she smirks. Little creep.

"Don't speak too soon."

"What do you mean?"

"Well actually it was going great at first, I made her breakfast and then I took her out on the bike and we ended up at this river in the middle of the countryside."

"Very romantic."

"I thought so too." I start, "Anyway, she saw this rabbit and ended up falling into the river trying to get close to it and I had to go and grab her."

"Oh shit, was she okay?"

"Yeah she was fine. Well, she scraped her leg up but that was about it. And then I um-" I stop myself and laugh, considering if I even want to share what I did.

"Oh no. What did you do?"

"I told her I love her." I can feel Skylar turn her head to look at me. She says nothing.

"She didn't really respond. She didn't say anything, but she was smiling. And the day had been so good and she looked so happy and I just got so caught up in the moment so-" Skylar puts her arm on mine to slow me down.

"It's okay." She says with a comforting look.

"I tried to kiss her, Sky."

"And what? She didn't want to?"

"She was leaning in at first but then she stopped. She pretty much didn't say a word to me the whole way back and then she mentioned that she would text me but I haven't heard anything. Basically I fucked it." I fake stretch and put my arms up, covering my eyes. Trying to hide from the humiliation.

"She loves you."

"I'm not so sure about that."

"She does. You know she does. But she can be... complicated. She's been through a lot."

"Yeah, join the club." She begins to giggle briefly.

"You think too much, Marcus. Just give her some time."

"I know."

"What about your dad?"

"He's just a prick."

"Nothing new there,"

"Yeah, I should've left that house a long time ago. Seeing that file yesterday just pissed me off so I had to let it out."

"You know you can stay here as long as you need."

"I appreciate that, I do, but it's not fair on your family."

"Oh come on. As if they'd ever ask you to leave."

"That's precisely the problem."

"Where you gonna go then?" She says with a pout.

"I'll stay here until I can convince Dean to let me crash with him."

"Ahh, so forever?" We both laugh and Skylar bounces to her feet.

"Well, I'll see you in the morning, loser" She says walking towards the door, but stopping to admire herself in the mirror first. "Ugh, so nobody thought to let me know that I still have mud on my face?"

"Mud?"

"Yeah, mum dragged me outside today to help her with the garden."

"Very exciting."

"I'm glad you think so, because you'll be here tomorrow."

"Fantastic."

"I'll leave you alone now. Oh and if Sienna finally calls you back, you can sneak her through the back door, it's always unlocked, just keep it down." She suggests raising her eyebrows and winking at me playfully. *Like I said, little creep.*

"I don't see that happening, but thanks."

"You never know what's gonna happen. Nobody does. I mean, you could end up a murderer... or a millionaire... or some kind of super secret agent. Or a -"

"You're rambling."

"Yes, I am. Night."

"Night, Sky."

Skylar smiles and holds up her middle finger to me before shutting the door unnecessarily loudly. The room falls silent once more, and I'm left alone with my thoughts. The most dangerous place to be. Sienna's smile when I told her I loved her is etched into my mind, but so is the look in her eyes before she walked away. Those fucking eyes. Fuck. I'm consumed by the thought of her. I'm tormenting myself.

I need to make her mine. To feel her body. I will. I have to. She's a drug. I check my phone again but still no messages. Should I message her? Will that make things even worse? My mind is reeling with so many thoughts that I can feel my head throbbing. What should I have done differently?

Has she been playing with me this whole time? It's possible. She's intelligent enough. I feel myself spiralling. The walls of this room are feeling smaller now than before. I send Skylar a text asking if there's any alcohol I can have, to which she responds by letting me know about some whiskey in the cabinet.

I make my way to the cabinet and grab the bottle, my hands shaking slightly. Walking back to the room, I pop the lid off and take a swig. And another. The burn of the whiskey slides down my throat, becoming a momentary distraction. I can feel the alcohol seeping into my system, dulling the edges of my thoughts. The room begins to spin, in a comforting way. As I take another swig, a heaviness settles upon my chest.

I can't shake the image of her; which is something that usually would be a blessing, a hobby, but today is a terrifying reminder of what I may have lost. Clawing at my sanity. I find myself typing and deleting messages, struggling to find words. After today I'm doubting if I've ever known the right words to say. In a bid to numb myself further, I take another swig, feeling the warmth of the alcohol spreading through my veins. I'm questioning everything now. Dissecting every conversation we've ever had. Considering if this was some kind of game for her. Manipulation of my emotions. The possibility is a twisting knife in my gut. Summoning the liquid courage, I begin typing. Pouring out my anger and emotions. My words spilling like a dam breaching. With trepidation, I press send and immediately shove my phone back into my pocket. Another swig. A very small weight now lifted from my shoulders.

CHAPTER 14:
NOT JUST THUNDER

I open my bag to start unpacking and the book immediately greets me at the top, staring me in the face once again. I take it out and throw it onto the bed beside me. I succeed at ignoring it whilst I unpack the rest of the belongings I need, leaving excess clothes at the bottom. I get changed into some tracksuit bottoms and a hoodie and sit back on the edge of the bed, checking my phone once again. Nothing. She has the power. I check the time, 12:27a.m. With nothing to do, I begin staring into the abyss, thinking again. I have to stop it. The only distraction left in the room is the book. Another thing constantly hanging over my head. I pick it up and fiddle with the lock that no longer closes. Why not? There are no pieces missing.

I start reading the story over again in another attempt to distract myself. I read the story a few times over, cringing at my handwriting but also flushed with a wholesome feeling, imagining my younger self sitting at my desk writing. Creating. I don't create anymore. As I read the story through another time I suddenly feel a strange sense of unease. I try to ignore it but I can't. Something feels off. Wrong. A chill runs down my spine and I quickly look straight ahead, trying to steady my mind. I look back at the page and read again. Wait.

'But then, disaster struck, 'Shy spider' stumbled and fell, injuring one of her many legs.'

The line has me thinking of Sienna, falling into the river. Even the character name. Sienna Saunders. It's all corresponding. I sit up straighter and I feel an intensity take over. Coincidence, it has to be. But I can't help but feel like I've discovered something significant here. My mind swirls with thoughts and possibilities as I flick my way back to the beginning.

'The animals were asleep peacefully in the village, when suddenly they were awoken by the sounds of rain and thunder crashing above the houses and a loud ROAR in the distance.'

Holy fuck. The bang. The storm. I've truly lost my fucking mind. My vision becomes blurry as I rush through the words. I look up and blink hard to focus my eyes again. Suddenly everything is correlating. I'm standing now, pacing. I focus on the names of the characters. 'Derpy Dragon', 'Baker Kitty', 'Sakura Fox'. Dean, Birdie and Skylar. They all match. This can't be happening. I shut the book and launch it onto the bed before grabbing my phone. My hands are shaking more than before. I text Skylar and tell her to come down. Waiting for her, I pace and pace, my mind hazy. I hear her footsteps down the hall and I open the door before she can reach it.

"Woah, you okay?"

"No, I'm really not, you have to look at this." Skylar rushes into the room behind me, a concerned look on her face. She picks up the almost empty whiskey bottle.

"Shit Marcus, how much did you drink?"

"It doesn't matter, look." I pick up the book and search for the line I need.

"You brought the book with you?"

"Yes. For fuck sakes will you just look." I point to the line about Sienna and she reads.

"Oh no, the spider broke one of its legs? And I should care because?"

"Sienna scraped up her leg today, remember I told you?"

"I remember Marcus, but Sienna isn't a spider." She says, looking at me like I'm an alien.

"But look, the name. The initials."

"Marcus, I think you need to sleep."

"Sky please, just listen to me."

"Okay, okay. I'm listening, calm down. Please, you're scaring me."

"Now read this." I proceed to show her the opening line of the story.

"You're fucking with me."

"I promise I'm not." We lock eyes and I can tell we're thinking the same thing. She grabs the book from me and begins reading intensely. Her eyes widen with disbelief as she too starts to realise that the book is becoming a lot more than just pen and paper.

"Oh my go-"

"What?" I interrupt in a panic. She looks at me with eyes filled with a mixture of fear and fascination.

"Read that." She points me to another line of the story.

'Sakura fox' scrambled desperately to protect the nearby flowers,'

"Gardening."

"Marcus, please tell me you're joking."

"Sky, I'm not."

"This can't be real. Things like this don't actually happen."

"You got a better explanation?" She looks into my eyes, her face white and her eyes empty. We stand in silence for a few moments, the weight of what we've just discovered sinking in. The room feels stifling and the air heavy.

"So what do we do?" She asks in a frenzy.

"We have to tell the others surely."

"But how is that gonna help?"

"I don't know, Sky. Believe it or not I've never actually written a magical future-predicting book before this one." Sky sighs and rolls her eyes, pulling out her phone from her back pocket.

"I'll tell them to come here."

CHAPTER 15:
'OKAY, YOU'VE OFFICIALLY LOST IT.'

"So let me get this straight. You've dragged us here in the middle of the night to tell us about a 'magical' book? You realise how fucked that is right?" Dean asks with genuine anger exuding from his slouched body.

"Come on man, you can't seriously sit here and tell me that's a coincidence." I argue.

"Yes. I can. You're fucking pissed bro, you're all over the place. You don't know what you're talking about."

"I'm tipsy, yes, but trust me I know what I'm saying."

"And what you're saying is batshit fucking insane." Birdie adds, looking at me like I'm some kind of nutcase. I rub my eyes firmly and pull my hands down my face in frustration, letting out an audible '*Aughh*'.

"It's just too far-fetched, Marcus. We're not living in a book. This is real life." Sienna adds with a discreet sliver of sarcasm. The one person in the room I want to back me up. I look at her, sat on the floor, her legs politely crossed and her hair a little bouncier than usual. A perfect little creation. I want to be angry with her, but I can't be. Not truly. Not seriously. How can I be when she looks like that?

"It is pretty weird though, you have to admit." Delilah says, finally speaking some sense.

"Don't give them pity, baby." Dean says, pulling her into his lap.

"I'm not, I actually think something might be up. How else do you explain the names matching?"

"Because when this loser wrote his stupid little book, we were the only people he knew." I shake my head and begin reading through the book again, trying desperately to find something convincing. Skylar peers over the book and points me to another sentence.

'Baker kitty' immediately got to work, using her magic to whip up medicine potions and remedies to give the animals strength in battle.'

"Birdie, what did you do today?" I ask, hoping for a correlating answer.

"Well, I met up with a load of girls from my college and went for tea, did some shopping, bought *THE* cutest mini skirt ever by the way... uhh ... then we just hung out at mine for a while. Oh and one of the girls surprised us with this cute little cocktail making class. It was adorable." Skylar and I look at each other immediately, our eyes piercing and our bottom lips practically on the floor. We soon notice that the rest of the room are looking at us like they're going to have us sectioned. I turn the book to them and point at the sentence.

"Convincing yet?" I ask, smugly, assuming the evidence is now undeniable. Wrong.

"No, Marcus. I made cocktails not magic potions."

"Obviously not, but it's the book equivalent." Idiots. I'm so passionate in my frustration now that I'm using my hands to act out every word I say. I can sense everybody getting fed up with us.

"Okay, you've officially lost it." She states, conclusively. I slam the book shut and throw it onto the bed. I don't know what else I can say. I'm not going crazy. Surely.

"You wanna know what I did today?" Dean says with an arrogant grin. I know the next thing out of his mouth won't be anything serious. "I turned into my dragon form and flew out of the city, on a search for a small village of animals to destroy with my fire breath. *Holy shit. No way. It can't be.* That's exactly what I did in the magical psychic book too! I'm 100% convinced." He stands up, Pulling Delilah up with him. He starts heading to the door and turns to me before making his exit. "Get some sleep, bro." The two of them leave the room, Birdie following after like the faithful minion she is. I turn to Skylar, feeling defeated.

"I'm sorry." She says, with a look of worry as if she'd let me down. "We tried our best. We'll have to work it out on our own." I motion to her for a hug and she burrows herself under my arms. I rub her back in a grateful way and squeeze her briefly.

"I'll leave you two alone. Night guys." Skylar whispers as she shuts the door extremely gently and the room falls completely silent.

Now what the fuck do I say? How do I fix this fuck up? Is this a *'play it cool'* type situation or a *'sit down and talk to me about your feelings for an hour'* situation? Luckily for me I don't have to give it much consideration, because before I can even utter a word, Sienna starts stepping towards me. Her tiny cold hands reach up around my neck and she attempts to pull me forcefully down. I play along, not knowing how this part of her game is going to end. I crouch down to her level and before I can even take another breath our lips meet. Her kiss is soft and tentative at first, but immediately ignites a fire within me. I feel my confusion melting away as our lips move together in sync. After a few seconds our lips part but our foreheads stay touching.

"I'm sorry about earlier, I-"

"Shh," I interrupt. "I want more," I grab her chin and pull her back in. I can feel the warmth radiating from her as our bodies press closer together. I walk forward, my lips not leaving hers, and push her hard against the wall. My arm instinctively resting on the wall beside her head, my body surrounding her, conveying my primal instincts to possess and protect. With each passing second, I can feel her surrender, her body melting. My sweet angel. I sense the intensity of my longing coursing through me. Lowering to her neck, my kisses remain tender, eliciting shivers that traverse her skin. The fragrance of her skin evokes a comforting familiarity, akin to the feeling of a home for me. Returning to her lips briefly, her tiny hand gripping my jaw amplifies my longing. Eventually, I reluctantly draw back, leaving us both enveloped in a hazy, smoky atmosphere.

I look down, smirking; she's looking back up at me, doe-eyed, flustered and giddy but her glare is so soft. Inviting.

"That was more fun than turning me down. Wasn't it, Sweet?"

"I'm just scared." She whispers.

"I'll go at your pace, wait for you as long as you need me to. But know this, sweet, you have nothing to be scared of." I take a deep breath before continuing, "I'd do anything for you, I promise." She smiles softly and I plant a kiss on her forehead.

"I should get home."

"Of course, let's get going."

"Marcus, my house is a few roads away, I don't need you to come." I scowl and laugh at the stupidity of her sentence before I turn around and grab my jacket, making a crystal clear statement. She pretends to be offended but her body language tells me all I need to know. She's welcoming my assertiveness with open arms. Seeking protection and security.

Waking up this morning, I'm on cloud 9. The room is filled with a lingering scent of alcohol and cigarettes, but for once I quite like that. A smile creeps on my face as I replay the moment with my sweet Sienna. Revelling in thoughts of her vulnerability. I thought I craved her before, but this is a new type of hunger. The door knocks.

"Are you up?" Sky asks.

"I am indeed."

"Mum's making sausage sandwiches, do you want an egg in yours?"

"Mm, yes please." My stomach is growling at the thought. I slip on a top and some tracksuit bottoms and make my way to the kitchen. The breakfast-smells of sizzling sausage and egg fill the air, causing my stomach to rumble beyond belief.

Skylar's mum stands at the stove, turning the sausages. She looks up and smiles warmly at me.

"Good morning, darling!" she greets me, "Sleep well?" I nod, trying to conceal my excitement.

"Yes, thank you. Breakfast smells amazing." I say with a yawn and stretch.

"Well, I figured you could use a good meal after yesterday." I take a seat on the end of the dining table next to Skylar who's staring at me with a devilish grin.

"What's up with you?" I ask.

"I may have stayed outside the door for a few minutes last night." She whispers.

"You little creep."

"Hey, it's my house."

The rest of her family join us shortly after. A real family breakfast. As I glance around the table, my eyes linger on Skylar's younger brother. His eyes are full of mischief and pure happiness. Good for him. I've always wanted a brother. The closest I have to that is Dean, and well that speaks for itself. I often wonder what it would've been like to at least have one sibling. Somebody to connect with in that way. To explore and banter with. As

Skylar's mum refills my glass of water she catches my eye,

"Everything okay? You seem a little spaced out."

"Yeah sorry, everything is fine. I'm just taking in the moment. I'm grateful for you all having me here. "

"You're part of this family, Marcus." I take a bite of my sandwich, savouring the flavours. After last night, the thought of a family of my own one day no longer seems entirely unattainable. We finish up eating and Skylar's dad and brothers start washing up the plates. I get up to help but Skylar's mum stops me in my tracks.

"Nope, I have a different task for you, darling-"

"Gardening?" I assume.

"How did you know that?"

"Sky was telling me all about how she was *forced into the insufferable activity of planting flowers* yesterday."

"Oh, she has such a hard life. The poor thing."

"Hey! It's not nice to gossip guys." Skylar snaps.

The sun is shining brightly, casting a warm glow on the grass and colourful flowers that adorn the garden. She clearly takes a lot of care in maintaining it. She hands me a trowel and points to a patch of soil that needs some attention. I kneel down to start digging. The earth is moist beneath my fingertips; well-nourished. With a determined grip on the trowel, I press its pointed end into the soil, feeling some resistance as I break through the surface.

A rich, dark layer of soil clings to the silver blade. I can't help but notice the intricate network of delicate, thread-like roots, weaving their way through the earth, silently nourishing the plants that call this garden their home. As I continue deeper the soil becomes increasingly loose and granular, easily shifting around my trowel and fingers. With each rhythmic thrust, the sound of the trowel slicing through the earth resonates, as though nature itself is harmonising with my efforts.

The sun casts its golden rays upon my back, warming my shoulders as beads of perspiration glisten on my forehead. As I dig further, the earth reveals small treasures hidden beneath its surface. Pebbles of various sizes and colours, ranging from smooth and round to jagged and angular, emerge from the depths. Clumps of tangled roots, like underwater creatures caught in a dance, arise with each deep excavation. These surprises serve as reminders of the intricate ecosystem that lies beneath the visible layers of this garden, functioning harmoniously to support its vitality and growth.

With each strike into the damp soil, I notice how the rhythm of my digging mirrors the rhythm of my own heartbeat, a steady but quickening pace fueled by anticipation. Suddenly I'm very eerily aware of my body and of every single grain of soil under me. I feel completely overstimulated and tingles flood me. My heart is beating much faster now, causing me to cough. I take a breath and steady myself. *Too much fucking alcohol I assume.*

I finally reach the intended depth. The hole I have excavated appears like a small abyss, awaiting the arrival of new life. With a gentle tap, I release the soil from the trowel's curved edge, allowing it to cascade back into its newfound dwelling. It settles neatly, making a soft thud of finality, ready to embrace the next seed or seedling that will soon inhabit this hallowed ground. Lost in my thoughts, I'm startled when Skylar's mom taps my shoulder gently. She has a mischievous grin on her face, her eyes sparkling with warmth.

"You know, Marcus, plants have a way of teaching us about life," she says, her voice filled with wisdom. "Sometimes they need a little extra care and attention to grow and flourish. And sometimes, we need to do the same with our relationships." Her words strike a chord with me, she's right. That's exactly what Sienna and I need. "You and your dad, you just need to talk things through. Most importantly he needs to get to know you." Of course. She's referring to my dad, not Sienna.

Why the fuck would she be referring to Sienna? You moron.

"You have the right idea, but unfortunately my dad doesn't do conversations."

"I feared that would be the case." She rests her hand on my shoulder and frowns sympathetically. "You know, Marcus, I meant it when I said you're a part of this family. Skylar had mentioned to me that you intend on heading to Dean's to stay. No offence to Dean, dear God the boy has been through hell and back, but I want more for you. This is your home now, and we're in no rush to get you out of here. Okay?"

"Thank you. I am gonna make something of my life you know? I won't be like my dad, no way. And when the day comes I'll repay you, all of you. That's a promise, and I don't break promises."

CHAPTER 16:
BITTERSWEET

Skylar and I arrive at the usual hangout spot to meet the others. They acknowledge us with their typical unenthusiastic and definitely high greetings. This place is a shithole but we love it. A train track surrounded by woods, next to a small graffiti covered tunnel. Our canvas. The track so rusted you would think it's abandoned, well it almost is. A train will pass by once in a blue moon, going who knows where, but that's it. A couple of ugly sofas, probably dragged here by somebody who was more than desperate to remove the disgusting things from their life, flattened beer cans, broken glass shards, discarded joints and cigarettes. All silently bearing witness to the various misdeeds we'd enacted here.

"Y'alright?" I mumble.

"Yeah bro," Dean responds, "I brought some cans." He pulls some spray cans out of his bag and throws one to me. We walk over to the tunnel and try to find an empty spot, of which there aren't many. The next best thing is an old piece we don't mind painting over. If I was entirely honest with Dean, I fucking hate graffiti. Not just the act of doing it but also how it looks. It's just not for me. It makes me cringe. But Dean loves it, and aside from Delilah, Dean doesn't really love anything. It's only fair that I make him believe I love it too. His eyes light up as he finds a faded spot to spray over, the only light ever igniting the dark corners of his soul. In these moments, my love for him overrides my strong disdain for graffiti. I want to join him in his realm, to share in the fleeting joy he oddly finds within these shitty painted walls.

"That looks nice, man" I lie.

"Cheers," He nods at me. "You come to your senses after last night? If you can remember it, that is."

"I wasn't even drunk."

"So you're still on this magical book thing, yeah?"

"I don't know man. It's just all too coincidental to me."

"You realise how crazy you sound though, don't ya?" I just ignore him and shake my head. I do sound crazy, yes, but I know I'm onto something. After a while we start walking over to join the others, sitting on the sofas and logs. Of course, my eyes immediately lock onto Sienna's face, which is being illuminated by the light from her phone screen. Her skin so perfectly smooth and her curls so elegant and bouncy. Each coil with a mind of its own, dancing whimsically with every move she makes. She looks up and catches my eye but looks back down straight away. Hm. I must be making her nervous, likely at the thought of being pushed up against a wall again with my tongue down her throat... and maybe something else.

Oh, my sweet.

I take a seat right next to her and place my hand on her thigh, but she brushes me off. *Interesting.* I guess she isn't in the mood for my advancements tonight. Or maybe the others being around is giving her stage-fright. The night progresses and the group falls into their usual state of intoxication, buzzing conversation mixed with laughter and the occasional argument. A single train passes through which adds an extra zap of rare excitement to the night. Four hours pass and our evening comes to an end. The others stumble off into the darkness and I hang back with Sienna. She's barely looked at me and I'm going to find out why. I walk up to her, as close as I can get without our bodies touching.

"So tell me, what's up with you tonight?" I ask.

"I'm just tired."

"Please, don't lie to me, sweet" She lets out a huff and crosses her arms, finally looking up at me. I'm making sure to soak up every drop of this sliver of eye contact. She's so cute when she pretends to be mad.

"I don't want to be with you, Marcus. Okay?" I raise my eyebrow and smirk at her. How pathetic.

"What did I just tell you? Don't lie to me."

"I'm serious. I don't want to be with you. I felt bad last night and I got ahead of myself." I don't say anything, instead my mind begins ticking. What exactly is she trying to do here? My smirk remains firmly glued to my face because no matter what bullshit she tries to blurt out at me, I know I have her now.

"Are you gonna say anything?" She asks. I don't, not yet. I want her to keep talking for a little while longer. "I'm sorry, Marcus. I don't want to hurt your feelings but I don't want any of this. I'm not in love with you and I just want you to be my friend again… and I really fucking wish you wouldn't have told me you loved me. It's stupid, okay? This whole thing is so stupid… I loved how I felt around you, I loved the thought of you but I realise I'm just not in love with you." I chuckle at her frantic rambling and crouch down to her eye level.

"Oh, Sienna. Using book quotes on me now? You must be head over heels." I whisper, my voice husky; dripping with a mix of amusement and faux sympathy.

"H-how did you know that was a quote from a book? You hate books."

"I know, but if you tell me about a book, I will force myself to read it," I pause to admire her angelic little face for a second, "I have to say I'm a little offended that I haven't been asked to recreate some scenes yet." I flash her a cheeky smile. "You must think I'm a fool." A flicker of confusion crosses her face, but it quickly fades, replaced by an adorable little defensive glare.

"What are you talking about? Are you even hearing me?" she retorts, her voice tinged with frustration and defiance. I love the taste of her resistance. It only fuels my desire to unravel her further.

"Loud and clear, sweet. But it's all bullshit." I say, my voice velvety smooth. "You see, I've always known you were playing hard to get, but it's cute how you thought that even after last night you could still toy with me. Make me believe that you're not interested anymore." She gulps and a sly smile curls on my lips. She knows every word out of my mouth is exactly right. I'm reading her like a book, and she's breaking character. This power play between us is intoxicating.

A game of control and manipulation that I'm fucking revelling in.

"Do you really think I'm that naive, sweet? That I wouldn't see through this?" I lean in even closer now, my breath warm against her ear. "You may be trying to push me away, but deep down, I know you want me *almost* as much as I want you." My words hang between us, the charged atmosphere crackling with tension. Sienna's eyes dart around, searching for an escape, for a way to regain control of the situation. But I won't let her. Not again. Never again.

"You're wrong, Marcus," she finally says, her voice trembling. "I don't want you. I never did." A surge of annoyance rises within me at her audacity, at her feeble attempt to deny our undeniable connection. She's merely testing my patience, attempting to gauge my reaction. But I won't let her win this battle. I chuckle softly, the sound dripping with arrogance.

"Sienna," I start, shaking my head. "I'll let you try your best to keep up the act, but we both know the truth. You can have a smart mouth and throw all the insults at me that you want, but unfortunately your body language is giving away all of your secrets." Sienna's eyes narrow, a mix of anger and resignation flashing across her face.

"You think you know me so well, don't you?" she scoffs, her voice laced with bitterness. "Well, let me tell you something, Marcus. You know *nothing* about me." Her words sting, but I refuse to let them derail me.

"You couldn't be more wrong, sweet." I trail my fingers lightly across her hand, relishing in the shiver that courses through her body. She makes no effort to stop me, of course.

"I know you like the back of my hand, and you have me in the palm of yours."
She pulls her hand away feistily and begins walking away in an adorable angry strut, making sure to brush me as she passes. I follow her, of course. I can't let her walk the streets alone, regardless of how much it may frustrate her. I'm certain she's aware of my presence behind her throughout the route, but I don't disturb her. She clearly has some shit to think through. We reach her house eventually and I stand straight outside the gate, lighting a cigarette. As she waits for her mother to open the door she turns around, a grumpy little look on her face.

"I can take it from here." she announces defiantly. I smile.

"I'll wait until you're inside."

CHAPTER 17:
DRAGON

I make my way back into Sky's house through the back door. Come to think of it, it's pretty dangerous for them to leave it unlocked like that. I sit down on the bed and roll myself a joint. I deserve one after today. I'll admit, I'm a little surprised that Sienna is still messing me around. But things are different now. I've had a taste of that power and no way in hell am I ever giving it back. She can play her little game all she wants, but I have a new strategy.

Just as I'm about to call it a night, Skylar bursts in the room.

"Hey, I know it's not my house but it would be nice if you would knock first." I burst out like an idiot before noticing that her face is etched with panic. I instantly know something is terribly wrong. I hastily stub out my joint and stand up straight, my heart pounding irregularly in my chest.

"What's wrong?"

"We have to get to Dean's, like now." Her voice is trembling.

"Why, what's happened?"

"His place is on fire."

"On fire? Are you sure?"

"Yes, Birdie just sent me a text. Delilah's there too." I shake my head in disbelief and try to gather myself.

"Are they hurt or?"

"She didn't say, Marcus. We just need to get going."

I don't ask anymore questions and we get straight on the bike. As we speed over there my mind is completely numb. A million different thoughts are banging around in my brain. I'm jumping every red light, swerving around every speed bump. The image of flames engulfing the place, consuming everything in its path. Is Dean okay? Is Delilah alright? I can't bear the thought of them being trapped inside an inferno. Skylar clutches onto me tightly, her nails digging into me, her fear palpable in the tight grip of her fingers. I try to reassure her, telling her that everything will be okay, but even I can't be sure. The panic in her eyes, the way her voice trembles, only adds to the anguish pulsating within me.

As we approach Dean's house, the sight that greets us is heart-wrenching. Flames dancing hungrily from the windows, smoke billowing into the night sky, casting an eerie haze over the street. The sound of sirens are filling my ears, serving as a chilling reminder of the chaos unfolding.

"Holy fuck, Marcus." Skylar yells.

We come to a screeching halt, abandoning the bike on the side of the road. Without a second thought, we sprint towards the blazing building. The heat hitting us like a wall, making it difficult to breathe. Each step forward feels like an eternity, the fear in my chest mounting with each passing moment. The lights from the fire engine are only making this feel more real. Firefighters in their bulky gear are already on the scene, battling the flames with torrents of water. The sound of crackling wood and glass shattering echoes through the air. I scan the building, desperately searching for any sign of Dean or Delilah. My heart sinks when I see Birdie standing outside, her face overtaken with worry, tears streaming down her cheeks.

"Birdie, are they okay?" I ask, my voice trembling with anxiety. She shakes her head, her eyes filled with anguish.

"I don't know any more than you do. I saw the flames from my window and got here as quickly as I could."

A sickening feeling washes over me, threatening to swallow me whole. I push through the disgusting crowd of people, none of them I've ever seen before, standing around watching Dean's house burning to the ground. I'm desperately calling out their names, hoping for any sign of their survival. My body moves on pure instinct, ignoring the heat and smoke, driven by the need to find them. Suddenly, I hear a familiar voice calling my name. I turn to see Delilah staggering towards me, her clothes soot-covered and her hair tangled. Relief floods every fibre of my being, but my joy is short-lived. She collapses into my arms, her body weak and trembling.

"Marcus," she gasps, her voice barely a whisper. "Dean... he's still inside."

My heart stops, the world around me fading into a blur. I can't comprehend the words she is saying. This can't be happening right now. Dean, my best friend, my brother, trapped in that burning house. Panic overwhelms me, immobilising me for a moment before my brotherly instincts kick in. Without hesitation, I dash towards the inferno, my mind on complete and utter overdrive. A few firefighters attempt to get in my way, but no force can stop me getting into that building. The heat intensifies with each step, threatening to consume me. The smoke chokes me, making it difficult to see, but I press on, driven by love and desperation. *Fuck, fuck, fuck.*

As I enter the house, the fire envelopes around me, licking at the walls and ceiling. I shout Dean's name over and over again, my voice desperate and pleading. The noise of crackling flames and the falling debris fills my ears, drowning out all other sounds. Time seems to stand still as I push through the flames, my body screaming in protest. But against all odds, I hear a faint cough from upstairs. A glimmer of hope ignites within me as I follow the sound. Through the smoke, I spot Dean, disoriented and struggling to breathe. Adrenaline fueling my strength as I race towards him, grabbing hold of his arms and dragging him towards the stairs.

In a complete haze, I manage to pull Dean out of the burning house and onto the front drive. His body is limp, his breathing shallow. Panic grips me as I assess his condition. His clothes are charred, his skin scorned; covered in soot and blistered from the intense heat. I frantically search for any signs of life, praying that he's still hanging on. He is, but only by a thread. Tears well up in my eyes as I realise the severity of the situation. I can't lose him. Not now, not like this. I dig deep within myself, finding the strength to keep going. Without another moment's hesitation, I scoop Dean's limp body into my arms and sprint towards the approaching paramedics.

The paramedics rush to Dean's side, their faces filled with concern as they try to stabilise him. The chaos around me fades into the background and I focus solely on Dean's well-being. The sirens wail, the firefighters continue their battle against the raging inferno, but none of it matters as long as Dean makes it through. Minutes pass by like hours. Before I know it Dean is whisked away in an ambulance, and I jump in beside him, refusing to leave his side. My eyes don't leave him. I don't feel myself even blink.

At the hospital, doctors and nurses spring into action, assessing Dean's injuries and working relentlessly. I'm left in the waiting room, my mind in a constant state of turmoil. Guilt gnawing and gnawing at me. If only I had been there sooner. Skylar sends me a text, finally.

Sky: Delilah's at home now. A little groggy but fine. Dean awake?

M: He wasn't awake in the ambulance but I don't know. They haven't told me anything yet.

Sky: I took your bike home. You need me to come get you?

M: Not yet. I'll let you know.

Hours pass, and the waiting becomes unbearable. I pace back and forth, my nerves on edge when finally, a doctor emerges from the double doors, his face a mix of exhaustion and concern. I walk straight at him, desperate for any news about Dean's condition.

"He's stable," the doctor begins, his voice soothing yet laced with caution. "But he's suffered severe smoke inhalation and burns. He's still in a pretty critical condition, and we're going to need to monitor him closely."

"But he's gonna live?"

"It wouldn't be fair for me to say that. We're going to do what we can, okay?" My heart sinks at the doctor's response. "There's nothing you can do for him right now. We have your details and we'll give you updates when we have them. Please, go home and get some sleep." With that, the doctor walks back the way he came and I'm left with no option but to leave.

M: You still up?

Sky: Of course. Should I leave?

M: Yeah. I'll wait out front.

I slowly wander out of the hospital, my mind in a whirlwind as I make my way to the front entrance. I collapse onto the bench and bury my face in my hands. How did it come to this? I replay the events of the night over and over in my head, torturing myself with the thought that I could have done something more to prevent this. The street is eerily quiet, the only sound being the occasional passing car. The only light coming from a single streetlight in the hospital car park. My mind becomes completely silent for a while. And weirdly, I like it, but the peace doesn't last long. *It never fucking does.* I hear the screeches of my motorbike coming down the road and I stand up sluggishly. The thought of Skylar riding my bike is cringe-worthy, but I'm too exhausted to care. Sky pulls up beside me and parks the bike, her eyes puffy and red from crying. She immediately launches at me for a hug, her presence offering some comfort amidst the chaos of my mind.

"How is he?" She asks, her voice barely a whisper.

"He's still in critical condition. The doctor said they're doing everything they can, but it's too early to tell." She stays in my arms for a few moments, not saying a word, and I can tell she's holding back more tears.

"You too tired to drive back?"

"Nah, I'll be alright, Sky. Come on."

We get back home and lie down on my bed for a long while. Letting everything soak in. My head is completely frazzled, as I'm sure hers is too.

"Marcus..." She says with hesitation, a concerned look on her face. "You don't think what happened tonight had anything to do with the book, do you?" I pause for a moment, the thought of it alone sending a chill down my spine. The book.

"It's just that, Dean's character was a dragon, right?..." I'm not sure I have the energy to handle where I think she's going with this. "Who destroyed the little village with...with fire." She looks at me and I look back. Her stare freakily intense. She's waiting for me to reassure her. I feel sick at the thought that she could be onto something. I start thinking about the events that have happened since opening the book, and now, watching Dean's house engulfed in flames, it's hard to ignore the possibility that the book is involved somehow. I sit up, the weight of the realisation heavy on my shoulders. Skylar watches me intently, waiting for my response, her eyes searching mine for any sign of understanding or confirmation. I take a deep breath, trying to gather my thoughts.

I grab the book and flick past the lines we had previously focused on. Skylar is now sitting up too, peering over my side. I begin reading aloud.

'At last, the Derpy dragon arrived, accompanied by his loyal sidekick who is 'definitely a Froggy'. The chaotic battle began and the village was soon awash with flames as the dragon breathed fire on the homes and shops'

I shake my head in denial.

"This can't be fucking happening." A sense of anger starts peeking through me.

"Keep reading."

'Despite their fear, the animals fought back valiantly, determined to defend their beloved home. All of a sudden, the dragon began losing energy, and fell to the ground, dead.'

"No. No. No." She squeals frantically. "That can't be right. That's not right, surely." She's standing now, holding me for stability and shaking like a leaf. I feel my entire body shut down. My throat dries out intensely. No words can leave my mouth right now. No words are even capable of forming. "Marcus.." A knot tightens in my stomach and I begin seeing stars.

"Fuck. Oh my god. I need to tell Delilah. Holy fuck. Dean is gonna d-."

"He won't, Sky. Not once we get rid of this fucking book."

CHAPTER 18:

DESTROY THE BOOK.

The moon shines brightly overhead, casting an ethereal glow on the garden. The air is thick with tension and anger as we wait for the flames in the firepit to build. I approach the pit slowly. The weight of the book feels heavy in my hands before I throw it into the rising flames. As I watch the flames licking at the edges of the book I can't help but feel like it's taking too long. The fire appears to be bending around the pages. We stare at it. Waiting.

"Fucking burn, you piece of shit." I murmur as I grab a stick, confusion painted across my face. I can feel the sweltering heat coming from the pit now. I use the stick to push the book deeper, hoping to progress the consumption. As I push the book deeper into the flames, frustration and desperation well up inside me. The book seems resistant to the fire. It's taunting us, mocking our attempts to destroy it. The pages flicker in the heat, but they refuse to turn to ash. I press the stick harder against the book, determined to force it to succumb to the inferno. But it remains unyielding. A sense of dread begins to creep its way into my heart. Now I'm pissed.

I drench the pit in water and snatch the book, taking it to the kitchen immediately. Skylar follows silently behind me. I rummage through the kitchen drawers to find a knife. And not just any knife. The largest one. The sharpest one. Once I find it I stab and stab at the book with no hesitation. Nothing. Not even a dent.

"How?" Skylar questions under her breath. The frustration and anger within me reach a boiling point as I continue to stab at the book, desperately trying to destroy it.

We move onto hammers, scissors, even attempting to drown the fucker. But no matter what we try, it remains unscathed. Each attempt is met with resistance, as if the book itself is fighting back. Skylar watches in horror, her eyes wide with disbelief and fear.

"I don't understand," she whispers, her voice barely audible. "How is this possible?" I shake my head in disbelief.

"There has to be a way, Sky."

We stay up until the early hours of the morning trying to destroy the book. Nothing works. After all we've put it through there's not so much as a scratch. I open the book again and try to find some answers in the words. Unfortunately for us, there are only a couple of sentences left.

'King 'Mint choc chipper' and Queen 'Milk 'n' cookies, deer?', who had been watching from the safety of their castle, waited for the dragon to die before emerging from the castle to inspect the damage brought by the dragon. Together, they closed the gates once again to protect their village.'

I read it through, studying every word, my exhausted mind ticking and ticking.

*'Together, they closed the gates once again to protect their village.'. 'Together, they closed the gates once again to protect their village.'. **'Together, they closed the gates once again to protect their village.'.***

Close the gates. My focus turns to the now unsealable clasp on the book. I try sealing it, but I know it won't be that easy. *Why the fuck would anything be that easy?*

"What are you thinking?" Sky asks.

"Look here, the very last line. What if the answer isn't destroying the book, but closing it." I suggest.

"Maybe if we find a way to close it before Dean dies we can change the ending of all of this."

"It's worth a try. But look," I flick the lock again. "It's not gonna shut. We're still missing something here." Skylar takes the book from me. Her eyes narrow and she begins biting on her thumb as she focuses on every word.

"Who's '*they*'?" She asks.

"The king and queen."

"*No shit.* I mean are they anybody's initials?"

"Well, the king would definitely be me. The main characters in my books were always based on myself."

"How very humble of you, Marcus." I smirk at her and we let out the first little laugh in a while. "Well, whoever the queen is, we must need her to close the book with you." I take the book back and think hard about the name. It doesn't take too long for me to realise.

"Fuck."

"What?" I look at Skylar before rubbing my hands across my face, knowing things just got a lot more difficult.

"It's Millie. The queen is Millie."

"Oh shit."

I flop back on the bed, head in hand.

"*Yeahh*, that book ain't getting closed anytime soon."

"Marcus, we don't have a choice."

"I know, I know." I sigh loudly. "It's fine, don't worry about it. I'll go and speak to her tomorrow. I need some rest first, it's like 7 a.m. You should sleep too."

"I will. By the way I have to be at Sienna's house at 6 today, you mind dropping me off?" She says with a defeated look. The mere mention of

Sienna's name brings a grin to my face. The suspense of not knowing when I'll get to kiss her like that again has been taunting me.

"Yeah 'course. What you going to Sienna's for?"

"She didn't tell you about it?"

"Tell me about what?"

"Marcus, she has a date tonight." I sit up straight and feel my face morphing into a concerned scowl. *A fucking date?*

"What do you mean a date? A date with who?"

"That boy from her science group. I saw you two hanging behind at the tunnel yesterday, did she not mention it?" I stand up slowly.

"Not a word."

Adrenaline begins to rise up through my body. Filling my veins. Every time I think I know how her game works, she throws something else at me. Oh, my sweet angel. So clever. But clearly not clever enough to know that letting another man touch her isn't something I'd ever entertain. The thought of it alone is enough to make me lose my fucking mind. But if she wants to take it here then I'm more than happy to play along. Clearly she needs a reminder of who she belongs to. I chuckle slightly, running my hand across my jaw. How exciting. I just hope my sweet doesn't have her confidence knocked too hard when her date doesn't show tonight. That fucker is going to die instead.

"Marcus I'm sorry. That's awful. I'll let her know I'm not gonna help her get ready-"

"No, no, no. I need you to go. I need you to do me a favour,"

"For fuck sakes, please don't get me involved in this."

"Just one thing,"

"Tell me what it is first."

"I want her phone."

"Okay, no."

"Oh come on,"

"That's too risky, Marcus. We don't need any more trouble right now."

"I'll take all the blame for it, I swear. I just need the phone... please."

"I don't know-"

"I need this, Sky. I really *really* need this... please."

"What are you even gonna do with it?"

"Cancel her date of course." She pauses for a moment, crossing her arms and tapering her stare.

"Marcus, we have bigger things to worry about," I stare at her and say nothing. My eyes pleading for me. She rolls her eyes and sighs dramatically. "Fine. But if she catches me you're taking all of the blame, got it?"

"Got it, pickpocket. Thank you very much."

"Yeah, yeah. Goodnight, loser." She says abruptly shutting the door as she slouches off.

"Night."

I take off my shirt and get into bed, closing my eyes instantly. As I drift off to sleep, Sienna is the only thing occupying my mind. *Nothing new there.* What was she thinking? After all these years I finally get a taste of her and she really believes I'm going to allow her to place her lips on some other man? Possible images enter my thoughts of some prick from her college daring to lay claim to what is rightfully mine. The thought of him looking at her in a class, or his hands on her body infuriates me to no end. A sinister smile takes over my lips. My mind has been shot into a frenzy. It's a possessiveness that scares even me, but I can't help it. She is mine. She belongs to me, body and soul. She knows that. But clearly she's underestimated me. Believed she could challenge me, push me to the very edge. Well then, let the games begin. I'll teach her a lesson she won't soon forget.

It's about to be a big day.

CHAPTER 19:
FINDING MILLIE

Waking up I feel incredible. Like an unstoppable force. I check the time. 2:13. With a burst of energy, I practically spring to my feet and put on my classic hoodie and baggy jeans. I grab myself a brand new pack of cigarettes, my bike key and of course, the book, from my bag before leaving the room. *I'm not usually a cigarette kind of guy, I prefer a good joint, but today I think I'm gonna need them.* I shoot a quick "Afternoon" to Skylar's dad and brother who are sitting in the living room, before making my way out. Sitting on my bike, I check my phone before heading off. One text from Delilah.

Delilah: I told Dean about the book when he woke up this morning. He left the hospital. The doctors and I begged him not to but he wouldn't listen, he's not doing good Marcus. Please hurry up and sort this book stuff out. My heart is breaking.

I take a big breath in before replying. I can't even imagine how she's feeling right now.

M: Don't worry. I'm gonna get this book shut, I promise.

It's a perfect day. The sky exactly how I like it, nice and grey. I'm riding smoother today than I have been recently. I'd almost gotten used to rushed, thoughtless driving after this week. It's a nice reset. Riding has always been my way of escaping. It's my graffiti. It's taught me a lot about myself. Patience being the most notable. Not to mention the ability to adapt to various terrains and the unknown. On the road, time seems to slow down, and every passing second becomes a treasure to be cherished.

As I throttle the bike, feeling the raw power pulsating beneath me, I notice all my senses awaken. The rumble of that engine reverberating through my bones. My bike really is a sleek, powerful beast. We both wear our scars proudly. We gained most of them together after all. There are scars etched all across my body that I've collected from my time with this thing. The road has become my sanctuary, my place of solitude. The scent of rain lingering in the air mixed with the faint smell of gasoline fills my nostrils. The hanging grey clouds adding to the atmosphere. Today is going to be perfect. I can feel it. I can taste it.

Arriving at Orchid's, I swiftly navigate into the car park, leaving my bike behind as I vault through the window. No time to explore today; I need that file. Traversing the scattered debris on the floor, I make my way to the office. Pausing briefly, I light up my first cigarette of the day, slowing down for a moment and relishing a few puffs. I open up the cabinet and search through the files. Bingo. Millie Devons.

I had almost wiped her from my memory entirely. From what I *can* remember, she was a posh girl. A quiet girl. It never really seemed like she wanted to be involved with us. I think she looked down on us. She never settled; just woke up everyday waiting for it to be time to go home. Orchid's was like one big waiting room for her. Once her dad's health improved she knew she'd be out of there. I even had a 'backup-crush' on her at one point when I had felt like I had no hope of ever being good enough for my sweet. *Clearly when I had written this shit book.* That was until my Sienna finally started to give me the time of day. As soon as she settled in her new life with her adoptive mother and started routine therapy sessions, she started to open up to me. Trust me. The greatest thing to ever happen in my life. Discovering my sweet angel. Where would I be without her now? The worst part is that I had found out after I left that Millie had been picking on Sienna. Now I have to go and ask this bully for help. *Kill me now.*

CHILD INFORMATION RECORD
GREAT BRITAIN

NAME: MILLIE DEVONS

DATE OF BIRTH: 03/12/2004

DATE OF ARRIVAL: 23/04/2006

REASON FOR ADMITTANCE:

TEMPORARY CARE

ANY FAMILY STILL IN CONTACT: YES

ELIGIBLE FOR FOSTER/ADOPTION

PROGRAMMES: NO

PERSONAL NOTES:

Millie was admitted at the age of 1 after her father fell sick and had to be hospitalised. Her father remains in contact but is unfit to care for her at this time. Once he recovers he shall once again obtain full custody.

Millie's dad has not yet recovered at the time of Orchid's childrens home closure and therefore she was transferred to Blackthorn childrens shelter on 09/12/2019

Blackthorn children's shelter. Maybe they'll have some information on where she is now. I make my way outside and start putting the shelter address into my phone. An 18 minute ride. I know nothing about this shelter, apart from the fact that the social workers in Orchid's had moved over there once it shut down. *And that it's probably a lot nicer than our home was.* I put out my cigarette and start making my way over there.

Arriving promptly, I park my bike. The area exudes a cosy, homely vibe. The streets are well-kept, and the people I had passed by appeared content and cheerful. As I take my helmet off, a few kids whiz past me on their bicycles, laughing loudly. I watch them whisper to each other and look over at my bike, an awkward, curious look on their faces. I snicker before acknowledging them with a nod of my head.

"You wanna give it a try?" I offer, gesturing towards the bike. Their faces brighten with delight, eagerly nodding in agreement. I hand them the helmet one by one, carefully explaining how to strap it on properly. They take turns sitting on the bike, gripping the handles tightly. I demonstrate how to rev the engine, guiding their hands and teaching them the basics. The thrill in their eyes brings back memories of my own fascination with motorbikes when I was their age. It's a moment of connection, where the boundaries between age and experience fade away, leaving us all united by the simple pleasure of a shared adventure. We laugh and chat as they ask me questions about my bike and share their dreams of riding one day. It's refreshing to witness their unbridled enthusiasm and optimism, a stark contrast to the darkness and uncertainty that has consumed my life recently. After some time, the kids reluctantly hand back the helmet and bid me farewell, still buzzing with excitement. As I watch them ride off on their bicycles, their laughter echoing, I wonder about their futures.

It makes me think about Sienna and I having kids of our own one day. I fantasise about it a lot. I know she'll be a wonderful mother. I imagine her tenderly cradling our child in her arms, her eyes filled with love and adoration. I envision the laughter and joy that would fill our home, the sound of tiny little footsteps from mini versions of us running through the hallways. Lost in this daydream, I'm brought back to reality by a gentle tap on my shoulder. I turn around to see one of my old social workers.

"Dot," I smile.

"What are you doing here making all this racket, love?" I reach out and give her a hug. I'm towering over her now which is a strange feeling.

"Oh my, you just keep going." She says, laughing and gesturing to my height.

"It's good to see you, Dot."

"It's good to see you too, sweetheart. Though I'm not too happy to see you riding one of these." She points to my bike with a disgusted look on her face.

"What's wrong with the bike?"

"Ooo, I can't stand those things. Much too dangerous. Anyway enough of that, it's far too cold to be talking out here, come inside." I follow Dot inside the shelter, greeted by a warm and inviting atmosphere. The walls are adorned with colourful artwork, and the sound of laughter and chatter fills the air. We keep walking and arrive at her office, a cosy space with a desk cluttered with paperwork and a worn-out yellow armchair for visitors. As I settle into the armchair, Dot pours us both a cup of steaming hot tea. Taking a sip, I feel a sense of comfort wash over me. Dot's presence has always had that effect on me. She was a subtle pillar of support during my time at Orchid's, always there to offer guidance and a listening ear. Like a grandmother I didn't have.

"So, Marcus," she begins, her tone gentle yet concerned. "What brings you here today? It's been a while since we last saw you. You must be wanting *something* from me." I take a deep breath, trying to gather my thoughts.

"Yes, I need your help, Dot. I've been looking for Millie Devons. Do you have any idea about where I could find her?" Dot places her tea on the desk, her gaze filled with compassion.

"Millie huh," she sighs. "I remember her. With those rather large glasses. She was such a quiet girl, always kept to herself, didn't she?"

"Yeah, I haven't seen her since I left but I really need to speak with her." Dot nods, her wrinkled face creasing a little deeper with the weight of her memories.

"Well, she moved out a few years ago. Managed to find herself a nice little apartment just outside the city. Last I heard, she was doing very well for herself." Relief and anticipation flood over me as Dot's words resonate. Finally, a lead to follow.

"Do you have her address or even a phone number I could grab?" I ask eagerly, my voice betraying my attempt to hide my urgency. Dot reaches into a drawer and pulls out an old notepad, flipping through its worn pages until she finds what she's looking for.

"Here," she says, handing me a slip of paper with her shaky, withered hand. "This is the address

I have. Just you be careful, Marcus. She's been through a lot and may not be too thrilled to see you." I take the slip of paper, holding it tightly between my fingers.

"Thank you, Dot," I say sincerely, meeting her gaze. "I appreciate your help. And uh, I'm sorry about the noise outside." Dot smiles warmly, her eyes crinkling at the edges.

"Oh, I understand, love. We all have our hobbies. Just promise me you'll be safe on that thing. I don't want to see you getting hurt."

With a nod of gratitude, I stand up from the armchair, slipping the piece of paper into my pocket.

"I will, Dot. Thank you again. It means a lot."

"And do come and visit more often, won't you? I've missed seeing your face around here."

"Of course."

CHAPTER 20:
A NOT SO WARM WELCOME

I linger outside the apartment building, taking a moment to enjoy my cigarette before retrieving the piece of paper to double-check the apartment number. No.2. I ring the buzzer and crack my knuckles while I wait nervously for an answer. I hear a slight crackle followed by a muffled voice,

"Hello." I clear my throat and put on my professional voice.

"Yes, hello. Delivery for Millie Devons." A beep comes from the speakers and the door clicks open. *Nice work, Marcus.* The entrance is perfectly white with beautifully smooth wood floors. The girl has money, that's for sure. Ascending the stairs, I make my way to apartment No. 2 and gently rap my knuckles against the door. Millie opens the door almost before I can finish knocking and instantly it's fair to say she doesn't look happy to see me.

"Marcus?" She scowls.

"Hey, Millie."

"What the fuck are you doing here?" She snaps, "How did you find my address?" She has a fire in her eyes, burning into me. The conversation is already off to a bad start and I'm only two words in. *Remember, this is all for Dean.*

"I'll explain, can I please come in?" She begrudgingly moves to the side and lets me in. I take a moment to look around, noticing the minimalist decor and the faint smell of vanilla in the air. It's clear that she has made a home for herself in this space. It's so clean that I feel like just breathing in here will make a mess. Millie gestures for me to sit on the sofa, her expression filled with scepticism. I can see the anger brewing beneath the surface, and I brace myself for what is to come. Taking a deep breath, I begin to explain

"Look, I know this is random and I don't want to make you angry, but Dean is in some pretty serious trouble and we're hoping that you can help us fix things." She laughs bitterly at me.

"You're asking for *my* help?"

"Yes, I am."

"The answer is no, now get out." Her words hang in the air and I rub my hand on my forehead briefly, trying to think of how I should navigate this.

"Just give me two minutes."

"I said get out."

"I know what you said, but I can't. Millie, please. We're adults. At least listen to what I have to say first." She sits down on the sofa opposite me, her arms crossed. I start explaining, keeping the story as short as possible. "We went back to Orchid's the other night and started searching through the old bedrooms. I found this book," I pull out the book and place it on her coffee table. "Once we opened it, there was a huge bang and since then the things I had written have been happening in real life,"

"I can't even believe I'm sitting here listening to this." She says, beginning to stand up.

"Look, the book has these characters, okay? And the characters correlate with everybody in the group, including you. Dean is the dragon and he's about to die, Millie."

"This is the dumbest shit I've ever heard-"

"You and I are the King and Queen, and the book ends with us closing the 'gates' after the dragon dies, to end the story. The gates correlate with this lock right here." I point her to the lock on the book and notice that she's looking at me as if I just parked my UFO in her living room or something. "I need you to come to Orchid's and close the lock with me before Dean dies. After that I promise I'll leave you alone."

"You're fucking psychotic. Now get out."

"Dean is gonna die! Don't you get that?" Millie scoffs, her face contorted with frustration.

"You think 'Dean the dragon' dying is my problem? After everything that happened, I don't owe any of you anything. You all left me behind, and now you expect me to swoop in and save the day? Unfortunately it doesn't work like that." I sit there, the tension between us discernable. Millie's eyes bore into mine, her anger simmering just below the surface. I can feel my frustration mounting, a mixture of confusion and resentment.

"Left you behind? *Oh* you mean we got adopted? I'm so terribly sorry for that, your highness."

"Fuck you, Marcus. While the rest of you were off having a great fucking time with your new families, I was stuck in that shithole all alone. Not a single one of you bothered to send me so much as a text message." I'm standing now. I didn't come to argue but I'm not accepting that bollocks for a second.

"You weren't ever interested in being involved with us anyway. Constantly acting like you were above us, remember? You'll never know what it was like for us, Mill. You had a home waiting for you outside that place, whilst the rest of us sat there wondering if we'd ever even have parents."

"My dad is fucking dead. He's dead, Marcus. But you wouldn't know that because you never bothered to find out."

Ah fuck.

I take a step closer to her, my voice laced with frustration.

"I'm sorry, okay, I'm really sorry. That's terrible and I can't imagine how that felt. But being mad at us isn't fair. We were kids, Millie. We got adopted for fuck sakes. I don't mean to be blunt but you can't seriously have expected us to be thinking about you at that moment."

"You guys were like a family to me. The fact that I wouldn't be on your mind is so fucked up and selfish."

"We had just been adopted, are you insane? The world doesn't fucking revolve around you, you know?"

"You don't understand, Marcus. You never will. You didn't have to watch your father take his last breath, or deal with constant reminders of what you lost. Just because you got your happy ending doesn't mean the rest of us did."

I laugh at her pretentious assumption.

"Of course, you're such a fucking victim. You forget that Sienna had both of her parents killed on the same day? Or is that not important enough because it isn't about you? Newsflash Millie, you're not the only one with fucking problems. "

"You're right, Marcus, I'm not the only one with problems. But I *am* the only one who had to go through it on my own."

"You know you have a phone too right? Why is it our job to reach out to you?"

"So when you guys all left to your new families, I was supposed to sit in that fucking home and message *you*?"

"That's what the rest of us did. What makes you so fucking special?"

"Okay, Marcus. You don't know anything about what I went through. You don't know how it felt to be forgotten and abandoned. While you were off living your perfect little lives, I was just trying to survive."

What a fucking drama queen.

I can feel my blood boiling, frustration seeping into every fibre of my being.

"Survive? You think the rest of us had it easy? You think being adopted meant rainbows and unicorns? I seriously don't know what you expected. Even before we left, you chose to isolate yourself." Millie's eyes blaze with fury, her voice trembling with intensity.

"I isolated myself? No, Marcus, I protected myself. I couldn't trust anyone, couldn't believe that anyone would truly care or be there for me. And you proved me right."

I stop myself from saying anything more. This clearly isn't working. I need to try a new approach. I step closer to her, my voice softer this time and filled with sincerity.

"I'm not here to argue with you. You can hate me and that's fine, but deep down you know we're still a family. Nobody leaves that place without a lifelong connection to each and every other person there and right now this isn't about us. Dean is gonna die and we can't save him without you." Millie's eyes remain filled with anger, her walls still stubbornly intact. But I can see a flicker of hesitation in her gaze, a sign that maybe, just maybe, she's considering my words. I continue, my voice pleading.

"This isn't about who was right or wrong, who deserved what, or who should have done what. It's about putting aside our differences and being there for Dean, because that's what a family does… Millie, please." She finally looks at me, the look in her eyes slightly less sharp than before. Some emotion pushing its way to the surface.

"I think you should leave." As Millie utters those words, I feel a mix of frustration and disappointment wash over me. Have I just fucked up the last chance to save Dean? *Think, Marcus.* I pull out the paper from my pocket and rip off a piece. I grab a pen that I spot sitting on a counter in her entrance and write down my phone number.

"Here," I drop the piece of paper on top of the book on the coffee table, "It's all up to you. You can stay trapped in your past, holding onto your anger, or you can choose to move forward. We have a real chance here to save Dean, to rewrite the ending to his story and we can't do that without you. You can choose to be a part of something bigger than yourself, or you can continue to sit in your fancy little apartment and wallow in your own self-pity." Millie stands there, her hands clenched tightly at her sides, her breath coming in shallow gasps. I can see the inner battle raging within her, the conflict between her desire to protect her ego and her grudging recognition of the truth in my words. After what feels like an eternity, she finally speaks, her voice barely above a whisper.

"I'll think about it."

That's good enough for me.

With that, I make my exit, closing the door gently behind. I check my phone. 5:29. Perfect. Time to deal with Sienna's little date.

CHAPTER 21:
CONSIDER IT CANCELLED

7:51. I stop outside Sienna's house once again and wait patiently for Skylar to emerge. *With any luck, she'll have an extra phone in hand.* Another cigarette destroying my lungs in the meantime. At long last the door cracks open and I vaguely hear Sky talking.

"Thank you for having me." Skylar shouts to Sienna's mother. I take a final drag from my cigarette and flick it onto the ground, carefully stomping it out with the toe of my shoe. As she rushes down the front steps I catch Sienna standing in the doorway; our eyes meeting for a brief moment. She's wearing a short, alluring black dress. The outline of her body on display. Emphasising her slender waist. I've never seen her in a dress like that. She notices me ogling her and gifts me with a disobedient little smile. She knows what she's doing. *Very brave, sweet.* Flaunting like that in front of me, knowing she's wearing it for another man.

We'll see if that smile is still there after tonight.

"I got it." Skylar whispers to me with a proud grin. Those three words are music to my ears. I keep my eyes latched on Sienna's whilst I wait for Skylar to get on the bike. There's a confidence in her eyes that I haven't seen in a while. Who knew she could get more irresistible? I make sure to give her a fake-stern look, just to remind her that she's in trouble, before slipping on my helmet and speeding away.

Once we reach the house, Skylar hands me Sienna's phone. A pretty lilac case on the back and a picture of her cat as her lock screen. I close the door, crack open the window slightly and sit down on the bed. The room dimly lit. I light up another cigarette; the least I can do to calm myself before the night I'm about to have. With a purposeful click, I unlock the phone, directing my attention straight to her messages. At the pinnacle of the list, a contact labelled 'Skinny jeans' catches my eye. This must be it.

S: **Are you still on for tonight?**

Skinny Jeans: Yeah sure.

'*Yeah sure.*'. Ungrateful bastard.

S: **What's the plan?**

Skinny Jeans: I'm down for whatever, just as long as you actually let me kiss you this time.

Excuse me? There's no way this fucker tried to kiss my sweet.

S: **How about that little Italian restaurant near college? I heard the food is amazing :)**

Skinny Jeans: Cool

S: **I'll book for 9?**

Skinny Jeans: Alright see you then.

Wow. Mr. 'Skinny Jeans' certainly seems like a bundle of fun. *Not that I would expect anything else from a man who wears skinny jeans of course.* Let's change up this plan a little.

S: Hey. Change of plan, I'm not really feeling like going to a restaurant. How about we keep it more casual instead?

I put the phone down and glance at the window waiting for a reply. Taking a long, deep draw of my cigarette, feeling the heat of the smoke trickling down to my lungs. The phone screen lights up.

Skinny Jeans: Yeah sure, what you wanna do instead?

S: There's this spot I like to go to sometimes to watch the trains go by that I think you'd appreciate

Skinny Jeans: Yeah that's fine, just send me the address.

I send 'Skinny Jeans' the location of the tunnel and tap out my cigarette. I change into my least favourite black hoodie and tracksuit bottoms. *No way am I getting my good clothes dirty for this prick.* Making my way to the kitchen I feel a surge of adrenaline building. Am I actually about to do this? Admittedly, the question doesn't linger for too long in my mind. *Yes, yes I am.* I instantly grab the knife I had found last night and slip it into my waistband before making my way out to the back garden. Opening the shed door, I flick on the light, scanning every object within. There it is, the shovel. I rush out, hopping onto my bike. My thoughts are too consumed to bother with a helmet. I speed toward the tunnel, the chilly night air whipping past me with a rough, sharp intensity.

I drop my bike just before I reach the tracks and make a pitiful attempt at hiding it behind a couple of trees. 8:58. I pull up my hood and wait. My adrenaline is building in a way I've never experienced. I can feel every single vein in my body. Everything is tingling. My entire vision is static. My body begins breaking into a cold sweat. My heart beating so fast that it can't be healthy. I remain in this state for a while. Waiting... and waiting. The tension in my body begins to settle slightly. I check the time. 9:17. Does this idiot know who he is supposed to be meeting? How dare he leave my sweet waiting in a place like this alone at nighttime. The cold nerves in my body morph into a burning rage.

S: Where are you?

I hold the phone waiting for a reply but keep my stare locked in front of me. *Ping.*

Skinny Jeans: Just left. Won't be long.

Just left? I clench my jaw and shove the phone back into my pocket. If only he knew how much easier he just made this for me. Continuing to stare forward at the opening to the tracks I remain completely patient. My body is frozen entirely. I'm unsure if time is passing by too fast or too slow. Either way, it's passing by, and I'm very aware that every second I wait is a second closer. *Ping.*

Skinny Jeans: Where you at?

Pure excitement floods every inch of my body. A sinister smile carving its way onto my face. My eyes dart around desperately, trying to locate him in the darkness. Found you. He's standing next to our sofas facing away from me. His eyes sealed on his phone screen like a moron. *Ping. Ping.* This is it.

I make my way towards him extremely slowly. My hand steadily making its way to the knife in my waistband. The closer I get the more I understand the nickname. His jeans are so skinny I'm surprised he even has any blood flow to begin with. I'm assessing him. Examining him. Average height with a muscular build. If the jeans weren't bad enough he's wearing a polo shirt at least two sizes too small. The cliché scent of his aftershave is getting stronger and stronger. He's certainly not a man even worthy of breathing near my sweet. *Or breathing at all for that matter.* I make my move.

As I grab his forehead and pull his head back, I feel the heat of his body in the palm of my hand. I quickly pull my knife from my waist and slice the side of his throat. I don't know what I was expecting, he'd just drop dead instantly? *Well it's safe to say that doesn't happen.* He wriggles out of my grasp, holding his neck. I watch the blood pour between his fingers and down his arm while he stares at me. The poor guy, he doesn't even know who his killer is. As I watch the red serpents grow from between his fingers, slithering down his porcelain hand and ever-whitening skin, his eyes become dreary. Before I even have time to gather my thoughts he lunges at me and goes for my knife, his grip easily escapable thanks to his blood covered hands. He tries swinging at me but barely makes an impact on my chest; merely grasping my hood and falling to the floor.

Face scrunched on the ground, wheezing, choking, drowning in his own blood. I feel sick, but I feel nothing. My hands are dead cold but my heart is beating faster than ever. I step back and watch his ribcage expand and retract with every noisy, bloody curdling, crackling breath he takes, knowing one of them soon will be his last. Not wanting to waste any time I roll that corpse onto his back, his eyes stay fixed onto mine yet his body is completely still. He can speak to me through his eyes, I can see the fear of death, the feeling of utter confusion as to who I am and why I feel the need to execute him this way. Stop. I can't waste any more time.

I walk around his still croaking body, his hands bent inward in impossible positions as his organs begin to fail. I stand directly above his head, his eyes now slightly veering off the right, focussing on nothing but death. Red foam drips from the side of his mouth as I watch his eyes glass over. I crouch down over him and bring my blade to his throat for the second time, look once more in his eyes, and slice. Deeper than before. I seem to bring him back to life for a mere second as he groans and begins to drown in his own blood pouring down his open throat from his arteries. His body twitches as I bring my blade to his throat again. Slice. And again. Slice. Each time his groans get quieter and quieter. I have never felt this way. The further I go, the more it feels like I'm doing this random, innocent man justice. Putting him out of the painful misery I placed him in. Well, *he* placed himself in. I just keep going. I can't stop myself. I am beginning to feel myself getting more comfortable doing what I'm doing. I take the bloodied blade and raise it to my eye level above him, and smash the knife deep into his spine through his throat. Silence. Just the sound of blood trickling like that small stream in the countryside. I leave my knife there, stand up, and grab the shovel I had brought along with me.

No kiss for you, *Skinny Jeans.*

I spend the next hour muddying my trainers, digging a shallow grave for the rotting corpse beside me, I walk back over to his body, now grey with death. Dark red blood dried up down the side of his face, his eyes still in that same position when I struck him with the final blow. I take his phone from beside him and use his fingerprint to unlock it. Quickly blocking Sienna before I put it in my back pocket. His contacts littered with other women. *Something my sweet should never have to worry about.* I unnecessarily take a moment to crouch down next to him and follow his eyes to where he was looking, just to imagine what it would be like to be in his position. To die in a foreign place, alone, with no one but a monster.

I grab his feet and try pulling him over to the eternal hole I dug for him next to the train track. He's too heavy, or maybe I'm just exhausted. Either way, I try a different approach, rolling him over, and over, and over again until I get him exactly where I want. He's trying to piss me off, trying to fuck me over, even in death. Leaving a trail of blood from where he died to where he now lies. *Does he think I'm stupid?* I grab my shovel and scoop up every speck of blood I can see on the floor to bury it with him. I tip him over the edge of the grave and he lands with a thud. I stare at him for a few minutes while he lay in a position impossible for a conscious person to put themselves into. Knotted limbs covered in blood, his nose pressed against one of the walls of the hole. Cringe. I don't hesitate to throw dirt over the corpse. One after another. Shovel after shovel.

I just fucking killed a man.

And the worst part is I don't seem to feel much.

Maybe I need time to soak it all in. I'm sure that's it. Or maybe *this* is it. It can't be, surely. Is murder just that simple? I keep waiting for my legs to give way or my heart to explode out of my chest. Something. Anything. But I feel pretty fine. I notice a slight tremble through my body but my heart rate seems to have calmed. My vision is clear. I just destroyed every memory this man has ever made and yet right now I'm wondering if I'll even remember doing it one day. I pick the knife up off the ground and slide it back into my waistband.

Do I just leave now?

What else would I do? I'm not sure. But walking away seems...wrong. I briefly sicken myself as a slight chuckle escapes my lips thinking about it. It's almost awkward. I take a look around, but I'm confused on exactly what for, before I make my way back to the bike. Rain starts pouring from the blackness of the sky above as I ride down to a small pond within the woods a few minutes away. I toss in his now-useless phone, checking the time before I do so. 11:27. Back on the bike. I arrive at Sienna's house and make sure her phone is clear from any blood or dirt before walking silently up to her living room window. Thankfully for me it's still open slightly. I reach my arm through, unintentionally budging the window open an inch more than before, and place the phone behind the sofa cushion. That should be enough to convince my sweet that she had just misplaced it.

After returning the shovel to its home and sneaking in silently through the back door, I get straight to washing the knife. I smother it in bleach, over and over again. The final drops of blood rolling down the plug hole. I've never put so much effort into washing up. *I fucking hate washing up.* Once I'm happy with it I place it back in the drawer and scramble to my room, locking the door behind me.

174

Pulling off my stained clothes and leaving them momentarily on the floor. I put on a pair of clean tracksuit bottoms and pick up the discarded clothes in a bundle. I walk out through the back door to the bins, making sure to shove the clothes deep into the bin bag. Taking a quick deep breath and feeling a huge sense of relief graze over me. Everything is covered. It's done.

Now, I'd better check on my sweet.

CHAPTER 22:
SWEET SURRENDER

I sit down on the edge of the bed, leaning forward onto my knees, and roll up a joint. The house is extremely quiet. My room feels tranquil. It's strange to see that life is just continuing as if I didn't slit a man's throat a few hours ago. I pull out my phone and call Sienna. *I know she won't answer, but at least she'll find her phone so I can bother her over text instead.* As expected, the phone rings a few times before she hangs it up. Text it is.

M: How did your little date go, sweet?

She responds much faster than usual.

Sweet: It was amazing. We're gonna get married and have babies.

I smirk at her audacity. I didn't know my sweet was a liar.

M: That's cute. Make sure you invite me to the wedding so I can burn the venue to the fucking ground.

I take a deep drag from the joint, feeling the familiar wave of relaxation wash over me. I exhale the smoke slowly, watching it swirl and dissipate into fumes. The scent of cannabis fills the room, mixing with the faint smell of blood that still lingers in the air. Which I'll admit is creeping me out slightly.

Sweet: How romantic.

M: Drop the act. We both know you're smirking and giggling at your phone right now.

Sweet: Attachment - 1 image

I briefly bite my bottom lip and smile as I see the image pop up. A risqué picture of her, still in that tiny black dress, sticking up a middle finger to the camera. *Well...to me.* I crack my neck and readjust myself. I know she's teasing me, and it's working.

M: You couldn't wait to show me that dress again, could you?

Sweet: Don't flatter yourself.

M: Just let me know when you want me to come and rip it off.

Sweet: That would be never. In case I didn't make myself clear, I'm not interested.

M: Prove it. I'll take you on a real date and we'll see if we can keep our hands off each other.

Sweet: You're so fucking arrogant.

I raise an eyebrow and smile. I can see her little character breaking once again. I finish my joint and stub it out, conjuring up my next response. Suddenly the phone rings.

"Are you gonna stop harassing me now and let me get some sleep?" She snaps. I laugh and lean back on the bed.

"You know you don't have to reply, right?" She says nothing in response. She's caught. "So you wanna tell me what this whole date thing was really about? And don't give me some bullshit story about you actually liking anybody else because I know it's a lie."

"You clearly can't take no for an answer so I had to make it crystal clear that I don't want you."

"Sounds like you're doing a very bad job at trying to convince yourself of that." I pause before continuing. "Talk to me. What's really stopping you, sweet?" The conversation falls silent for several seconds and I can almost hear her pretty little mind ticking through the phone.

"I'm in love with you. Like really *really* in love with you." I hear her vaguely whimpering through her words and her voice beginning to tremble.

"I know you are. So what's all this about then?"

"Marcus, I can't be with somebody I truly love. I just can't. I won't. I loved two people in my

179

life and both of them left me on the same fucking day. But I can't escape you. I'm doing everything I can to move on from you. Nothing I try works." My poor angel, now almost sobbing down the phone. Her voice filled with pure pain. I can't bear to hear one more syllable without having her in my arms.

"I'm coming over to listen, okay? Unlock the door for me and I'll be as quick as I can. Please."

"Fine," she whispers before hanging up. I slip into a plain T-shirt and race over to her.

Sienna opens the door, biting her fingers nervously, her face wet with tears. It stings me to see her like this. Without second thought, I scoop her into my arms, her legs wrapping around me. I close the door with my elbow whilst holding her tight, feeling her tension as she sinks herself into me.

"Let it out, sweet. I'm here, I've got you. I've always got you." With that, her soft whimpers turn into hard, deep cries. Her body jolting with every sob. Her tears, relentless, find refuge in the fabric of my t-shirt. I hold her closer, wanting to absorb some of her pain, to bear the burden with her. I cup the back of her head with my hand, her beautiful curls spilling through my fingers, rubbing her back slowly with my other hand. We stand in the doorway for what feels like an eternity, her cries echoing through the silent house.

Slowly, I begin carrying her to the stairs and up to her bedroom, shutting the door carefully behind me. Trying my best not to change her position, I sit down on the edge of the bed. I continue to hold her tight: to let her cry, making sure not to interrupt her. Feeling the warmth of her tears against my chest as she clings to me, seeking shelter from the storm of emotions consuming her. Her cries gradually begin to subside, replaced by softer sniffles and shaky breaths. I glance down at her, the dim light of the room illuminating the tear stains on her cheeks. I delicately brush away a single soft curl, stuck to her damp face. She remains clinging to me, still seeking solace in the midst of her vulnerability. I hold her close, pressing gentle kisses against her forehead. Her eyes and cheeks now puffy, but still so incredibly beautiful. An entirely flawless being.

"You ready to talk to me?" I ask, caressing her cheek. She nods briefly and takes a breath, followed by a couple of precious little sniffles. Her wide eyes, flushed with tears, looking right up at me.

"I'm terrified of loving you." she whispers, her voice trembling. She searches my face, desperate for reassurance and understanding. My body tightens as I contain my emotions.

"Sienna, I'm never gonna leave you." I assure, a whisper against her skin.

"You can't promise me that. Nobody can. Just look at what's happening with Dean right now." Leaning in closer, I gently press away a tear from her cheek with the back of my hand. Her lip begins to shake and she breathes in hard through her nose. "I miss my parents so much, Marcus. I can't miss anybody like that again." I pause and think carefully about my words.

"You're right, I can't promise you that." I start, looking deeply into her eyes, "But what I can promise, is that every moment I have left of this life will be devoted to loving you." A single tear trickles down her cheek, rolling onto her chin and forming a single gorgeous droplet, as she listens attentively. "Sweet, as long as I have breath in my lungs and a beat in my heart, everything I do is for you. You *are* my life, and I'm not going anywhere."

The air in the room feels heavy with the intensity of the moment, as if time itself has paused to witness this pivotal exchange between us. Without saying a word, Sienna leans in, her trembling lips brushing against mine. It's a gentle, hesitant kiss, filled with both longing and fear. I can taste the saltiness of her tears mixed with the sweet warmth of her breath. At this moment, everything else fades away. All dissipating into nothingness. There is only Sienna, and the overwhelming rush of love and obsession coursing through my veins. I respond to her kiss with tenderness and passion, pouring every ounce of my devotion into that single, electrifying touch. Our souls are intertwining, finding solace and strength in one another. My entire being and existence depending on the beautiful angel sitting in my lap. Sienna's fingers thread through my hair, pulling me closer, deepening the kiss. It becomes more urgent, more desperate, as if we're trying to consume each other's pain.

In this stolen moment of raw vulnerability, I whisper against her lips, "Is this finally a sweet surrender?" She smiles and rests her forehead on mine before answering.

"I don't know, I quite enjoy playing hard to get." With that, I smile wide and pull both of our bodies back onto the bed, squeezing her tightly and planting hundreds of playful kisses over her body.

We lay together in silence for a while. My fingers tracing every curve.

"You're still in trouble, you know?" I say, breaking the silence and giving her a faux mean glare. Her face drops slightly, a nervous glint in her eyes.

"I lied about the date. I was just trying to find somebody else I could be with and put my focus on. I needed a distraction and I couldn't even get that. The guy fucking stood me up." She looks away from me, almost embarrassed. Her poor little face, sheepish and drained. "He even blocked my number."

Fuck it.

"He didn't stand you up, sweet." She looks back over to me, scrunching her eyebrows.

"What do you mean?" I draw her focus to the dried patches of blood still remaining on my hands, staring intensely at her in anticipation of her reaction. Her eyes widen in shock and disbelief as she looks down. Her mouth opens, intending to say something, but no words come out. Fear and confusion dance across her face, and I can see the wheels turning in her mind as she tries to process the horrors I've just revealed. I watch her body freeze, her breath caught in her throat.

"Fuck Marcus, you ki-"

"Don't think about it, sweet." I interrupt, "You'll make yourself sick."

"That's beyond crazy. You can't just go around killing people! Why would you do that? How?-"

"I told you, I'd do anything for you," I pause, "You're *mine*, sweet. Any man who tries to take you from me is a threat and I will eliminate that threat." Sienna doesn't respond. The look on her face is unreadable. I'm not worried, I know she didn't care about him. I sit back up on the edge of the bed, leaning forward, and place a comforting hand on her thigh. "It was over quickly, I promise."

"Because of a date? Have you lost your mind?" I stand up and face her.

"If I didn't do something, that fucker would've tried to kiss you, sweet…for the *second* time." I say, raising an eyebrow. *Busted.* She looks up at me, sucking in her bottom lip. Guilt written over her face as though she's being reprimanded.

Which she is.

"I stopped him the first time,"

"There shouldn't have been a fucking first time. What if you couldn't stop him the second time? What if he wanted more than a kiss? Huh?" I challenge. She doesn't reply. "Let's call it even, shall we?" She remains frozen in place, her eyes glaring up at me. A hollow expression on her face. Almost as if she's afraid of me, and if I'm honest I quite like it. I wait a few more seconds for a response that doesn't come, before letting out a big sigh.

With slow, deep footsteps I make my way to her bedside table and open her pyjama drawer. I sift through her collection, picking out a cosy little beige set. The act of carefully selecting her sleepwear feels strangely comforting. Intimate. As if I'm taking a small step towards creating a sense of security and stability for the both of us. I turn around to face Sienna, still sitting on the bed, her eyes locked on me with a mix of confusion, disbelief, and a hint of fear.

Who knew fear would be an expression I'd enjoy seeing on that sweet face?

"Come on," I coax gently, holding the pyjamas in my hand, "Let's get you ready for bed." She hesitates for a moment, her eyes oscillating between the offered garments and I. I can see the internal struggle, weighing her emotions against the grim reality of what I had just revealed. Apprehensively, she climbs up off the bed and stands in front of me, fidgety and timid. As her hand reaches out for the pyjamas, I intercept, placing them beside me on the bed. "Turn around," I instruct. She complies, her back now turned to me.

I carefully lift up her hair and unzip the sexy little black dress. The soft fabric falls to the floor, pooling around her feet, leaving her in nothing but her underwear. My fingers skillfully trace down her body, revealing the vulnerable beauty hidden beneath the fabric. Her body slowly unveiled before me, a canvas of temptation, each layer discarded with reverence as if unwrapping a precious gift. I swallow hard, trying to suppress the rush of torturing desire that threatens to consume me, reminding myself that this moment is about comforting her. Once my hands reach her hips I tighten my grip and spin her back around to face me. I keep my hands lingering on her hips for a moment whilst her beautiful doe eyes glance up uncertainly at me.

Picking up the pyjama top, I gently guide her arms through the sleeves, the soft fabric embracing her delicate frame. Pushing her down onto the bed's edge, I kneel before her, sliding the pyjama bottoms up her legs, cherishing each inch of her body. The fabric, velvety against my touch, reminding me of her innocence I'm slowly beginning to take from her. I look up, meeting her eyes as I pull the bottoms up to her thighs, the boundary of my touch marked by the bed's edge. There's a tangible, sensual tension between us, and for once, I can tell I'm not the sole participant in this unspoken exchange of desires. She lets out a soft sigh, her eyes fluttering closed as she leans back lewdly onto the bed. Her back arched.

Adding to my mental list of reasons why she has me entirely mesmerised.

She raises her hips as I pull at the bottoms once more, knotting the waistband to complete the ensemble. Admiring her in those adorable pyjamas, a surge of protective satisfaction washes over me. Sienna opens her eyes, her gaze filled with a mixture of vulnerability and desire. Without saying a word, I lean over her, my lips hovering just inches away from hers. The anticipation hangs heavy in the air as we both feel the electricity between us. I press my lips against hers, starting off slowly, savouring the softness and warmth of her mouth. It's a gentle kiss, filled with tenderness and a yearning that only grows stronger with each passing second. As our lips move in sync, I feel her body relax against mine, a whispered moan escaping her mouth. The kiss deepens, becoming more passionate and intense.

My hand explores her body, tracing along her spine and down to the curve of her waist. The fabric of her pyjamas feeling impossibly soft against my fingertips. I can feel the heat radiating from her body, matching the fire that courses through my veins. I stop myself. Nothing more can happen tonight. Not yet.

I don't want it to be that easy.

As I pull away from Sienna's lips, I can see the confusion and desire etched on her face, still sprinkled with a hint of genuine fear for me. I know that she wants more, *bless her heart*, but I can't give her what she's craving just yet. I want to build her up. I sigh and take a moment to be in my thoughts. Looking down at her in this state is forcing me to realise just how terribly twisted I have become, I'm completely relishing in the power I hold over her. Knowing that eliminating that loser has gained me an extra degree of intimidation and control over my sweet is a very dangerous weapon in my arsenal. At long last, this little game she had me playing has been fully turned against her. I have her exactly where I want her now. Vulnerable and afraid, yet still entirely drawn to me. I resist the urge to smirk and instead focus on the task at hand.

I lift the duvet cover, inviting her to slip inside, ensuring it wraps snugly around her. I position myself behind her, spooning her body, and gently wrap my arm around her waist.

"Marcus, what if you get caught?" She whispers suddenly. I pull her body closer to me before responding.

"I don't get caught." The warmth of our bodies mingling creates a comforting cocoon. Sienna remains silent, her breathing shallow and uneven, as her mind processes the conflicting emotions coursing through her. I nuzzle my face into the crook of her neck, planting soft kisses along her collarbone, savouring the sweet taste of her skin. Every touch and caress is deliberate, calculated to keep her off-balance.

"Sleep tight, sweet" I whisper gently into her ear. Pressing a firm kiss to her temple; relishing in the way she nestles closer to me in response. It doesn't take long for my exhausted little sweet to drift off. I watch over her, my fingers gently stroking her hair as she rests. Her body is entirely peaceful, as it should be.

I close my eyes too and in the quiet darkness of the room, I find myself drifting into a restless sleep. Momentarily, a surge of self-awareness washes over me as I question my motives for the first time. Two foreign sensations that I seldom experience. It's almost as if the line between protector and predator is becoming slightly blurred in my mind. I'm jolted from the precipice of slumber, a cruel reminder that peace eludes me. The image of my violent act replays like a dreadful loop, each detail becoming more vivid with every repetition. I glance down at my blood-stained hands as the weight of what I have done bears down upon me.

But instead of remorse tugging at my conscience, there is an unsettling absence of emotion, a void where regret should reside.

As the night wears on, I find myself trapped in the clutches of insomnia. There is a disturbing calmness that's eating at me. What does it say about me as a person, as a human being, that I could commit such a horrific act and feel nothing but a sense of satisfaction, tinged with regret over my own naiveté? That I could slice a man's throat several times, watching the blood drain from him and still feel okay. I find myself hoping, praying even, that some semblance of guilt will eventually find its way into my heart. That perhaps there is still some flicker of humanity buried deep within my soul, struggling to surface amidst the darkest recesses of my consciousness. It is an odd desire, to long for the torment of remorse. But in its absence, I am left wondering if I have truly lost myself in the process of this monstrous act.

I feel really fucking good, and there's a lot wrong with that.

CHAPTER 23:
A SLICE TO DIE FOR

After an hour or so of successful sleep, I'm awoken by Sienna's disgraceful and frankly terrifying alarm. *I guess 'bad taste in alarm noises' will be the first and only negative I can give her.* I reach over to turn it off before placing a kiss on her forehead.

"Good morning, beautiful." I start, smiling at her with pride "How did you sleep?" She delicately rubs her eyes, with clean hands, before turning to snuggle into me.

"Good actually," she replies, her voice soft and drowsy. "I slept right through." I can't help but chuckle at her response, finding her innocence charming, even in light of my newly shared secret.

"Because I'm here?" She shrugs me off and sits up, yawning and stretching her dainty arms out wide.

"No, because you exhausted me." She retorts with a hint of attitude.

"Well I'm glad you slept well, you always should."

"What about you?" She asks softly, concern lacing her voice. "Did you sleep well?" I offer her a faint smile, masking the internal tumult that has plagued my mind all night.

"I never sleep well." It's a half-truth. Sleep has always eluded me, but last night felt like a punishment rather than a natural state.

As I begin to get out of bed, my phone pings.

Sky: Get here. Right fucking now.

Well, that's not very polite.

I sigh in annoyance as I read Skylar's demanding message. Despite the urgency in her tone, I can't find it in me to muster any enthusiasm for her problems. With minimal effort, I reply with a curt message, 'On my way.' before tossing my phone onto the bed and turning my attention back to Sienna, who is now awake and watching me curiously. I can see the concern in her eyes, but I quickly dismiss it as irrelevant.

"I'm sorry sweet, I have to rush off."

"What's wrong?"

"Nothing," I reassure her. "Sky just needs my help with something. You'll be at Delilah's tonight, right?"

"Yeah of course." I quickly get myself ready and grab my bike key, giving sienna a kiss on the forehead before making my way out.

Opening the door, I'm immediately greeted by Sky's mum and dad decorating. Both with their arms full of vibrant streamers and colourful balloons. A wave of cheerful chatter and the sweet aroma of freshly baked cake catching me by surprise. I think about Sky's text. I must have forgotten somebody's birthday.

"Afternoon, darling!" Her mum shrieks, embracing me in a hug. "How does it look?"

"It looks amazing, you guys did a great job."

"Thank you, Marcus. I've got a lovely birthday lunch coming up too, you're going to join us aren't you?"

"Definitely." I flash her a smile before walking through to my room.

As I open the door I'm startled to see Sky sitting on my bed, angry as angry could be. I raise an eyebrow, puzzled by her rage and shut the door behind me.

"Care to explain?" She snaps, holding out her phone. I take Sky's phone from her outstretched hand and glance at the screen. My heart skips a beat as I read the headline:

'Local Man Reported Missing.'

My eyes narrow in disbelief as I scroll through the article, detailing the disappearance of the man I had killed just last night. *Fuck me, that was fast.* A picture of his smug little face staring back at me. I look up from the phone and meet Sky's intense gaze.

"I'm sure I don't need to tell you this, but that's the man Sienna was planning to go out with last night." She continues. I shrug nonchalantly.

"So what?"

"Really, Marcus? That's all you've got?"

"What do you want me to do? Break down in tears?"

"Cut the shit. What did you do?" Sky's accusing eyes bore into mine, demanding an explanation that I'm not ready to give. I meet her gaze, my voice calm and steady,

"I did what I told you I was gonna do, I cancelled the date." I remain impassive, unwilling to give her the satisfaction of seeing me squirm. She scoffs, a bitter laugh escaping her lips.

"Cancelled the date, huh? That's a clever way of putting it." She sneers, "You killed him. Didn't you?" I take a deep breath and rub my face briefly. The weight of the situation is slowly resting on me.

"Look, I took care of it. That's all you need to know." I walk over to the window and light up a cigarette, Skylar's eyes burning a hole through the side of me. I take a drag, trying to maintain my composure.

"How could you?" I turn to face her, looking her directly in the eye.

"What did you expect me to do, Sky?" I ask, my voice calm and composed. Her brows furrow in anger and disbelief.

"You don't just get to play God, Marcus," she snaps, her voice filled with frustration. She covers her mouth with her hands as her emotions begin to surface. "How did you do it?"

I blow some smoke slowly from my mouth, observing it closely as it swirls. My mind transported back to the moment the knife pierced through his throat. I can feel it again. Hear it again. Smell it again. The crack of his spine. The blood soaking into my skin; rising up through my nostrils. His contorted corpse on the soil. Feeling his life drain into my hands.

Holy fuck, I wish I could do it again. Over and over.

Isn't that disgusting? Insane? Yes. But it's the truth. I don't like to run from the truth. Most of the time. I fade out of my daydream and catch myself unintentionally smiling.

"You're sick!" Skylar seethes at me. "How did you do it, Marcus?" Her voice is so shrill it's starting to piss me off.

"Do you really wanna know?" I ask with a smirk as I walk up close to her, my cigarette wobbling between my fingers.

"I grabbed his face. I pulled his head back." I pause for dramatic effect, "And I slit his fucking throat."

Skylar's jaw drops to the floor, her face now void of colour. Tears beginning to fall like silent raindrops.

"You won't get away with it."

"Why's that? You gonna turn me in?" I taunt. She won't do anything, I know that. She's not that stupid. I'm met with no response, her eyes now streaming with tears. I meet her gaze with an unsettling calmness, my voice dripping with a detached yet sinister elegance. "Sky, don't worry about it. It's over." I remark coldly, turning away from her to take another drag of the cigarette, the acrid smoke curling around my words. "I did what I needed to do to protect Sienna."

Skylar scoffs incredulously, her voice laced with a mix of bitterness and desperation.

"Protect her? Is that what you call it? Taking matters into your own hands, playing judge, jury, and executioner?" A flicker of pain flits across Skylar's tear-stained face, a reflection of the fracture in our friendship. She takes a step back, her resolve waning in the face of my unwavering conviction. "You're evil, Marcus." she whispers, her voice barely audible through choked sobs.

"And Sienna is innocent, pure," I say, my tone now softening but no less determined. "She needs me, whether she likes it or not, and if I have to become the villain to keep her safe then that's what I'll do." Skylar shakes her head, tears surging down her face as her voice trembles with a mix of anger and hurt.

"You can't just justify your actions like that, Marcus. That was someone's life you took."

"And I'd do it again." I state firmly, my voice devoid of remorse or regret. The room seems to grow colder, as if the weight of my actions are sucking the warmth out of the air.

"Now, if you don't mind, I'm gonna go and enjoy some birthday lunch." I say, leaning in close to her. "Pull yourself together, Sky."

I pass her slowly and leave, slamming the door behind me. abandoning the tension and heavy air from the room.

As I make my way down the corridor, a burst of energy comes charging toward me in the form of Skylar's younger brother. His face lights up with an exuberant smile, proudly sporting a sizable 'Birthday Boy' badge on his jumper. The weight of whatever I had just been absorbed in discussing dissipates instantly as I mimic his infectious grin and crouch down to his level.

His infectious spirit rubbing off on me.

As he reaches me, I catch him in my arms and toss him high in the air. His laughter echoes through the hallway as I spin him around, feeling my smile carving into my cheeks and aching my jaw. Lowering him back down to the ground and setting him back on his feet, he grins up at me, the shadows in his dimpled cheeks bright against his pale skin.

"Look at you, little birthday boy!" I exclaim, my voice filled with genuine happiness. "You're getting bigger by the minute."

"I'm six now!" He announces.

"You know what being six means, right?" I ask, a mischievous grin forming on my face. His eyes widen with anticipation, his voice bubbling with excitement.

"What? What does it mean?"

"Well," I begin, placing a hand on his shoulder. His face lights up with excitement as he remembers an old promise, and he begins to bounce on his feet.

"You're gonna get me a bike just like you?"

"Absolutely," I say, ruffling his hair. "Pick out whatever bike you want and I'll get it for you, yeah?"

"Really? I can pick any bike I want?" he squeals, his voice filled with disbelief and excitement. I can't help but laugh at his enthusiasm, a sound that feels rare and foreign on my own lips.

"Yup. Any one you want, little man."

"I want a black one just like yours!"

"A black one huh? Excellent choice." With a gentle pat on the back, I guide him toward the living room. "Alright, birthday boy, let's go tuck into some birthday lunch." I suggest, winking at him. He nods eagerly and reaches out to grab my hand, his small fingers intertwining with mine.

As we enter the living room, Skylar's parents, adorned with abundant smiles, beckon us to join them at the beautifully decorated dining table. I lead her brother to his designated seat at the head of the table and sit down next to him. The room is filled with the aroma of delicious food, and I can't help but be drawn to the spread in front of me. The table cluttered with various sandwiches, sweet treats and finger food. As I begin to serve myself, Skylar takes a seat opposite me, her face red and blotchy. *This is going to be fun.*

"The roast potatoes are incredible!" I declare, nodding my head in approval to Sky's mother.

"Thank you, darling. They're one of my specialties." Skylar spitefully grabs a roast potato and takes a bite, staring through me.

"Mm!" She exaggerates. "You're right, Marcus. The seasoning is killer." I raise an eyebrow and connect to her gaze.

Safe to say, if looks could kill, I'd be in the ground with Skinny Jeans right about now.

She takes a huge scoop of roast potatoes, her eyes still fiercely fixed on me as if daring me to respond. A smirk plays on my lips as I take a sip of my drink, keeping up with the charade.

"Woah, don't get carried away there, Sky. You wouldn't wanna take on more than you can handle."

Her dad quickly interrupts, laughing. "No need to worry about that son, the girl can eat. There's never food left on her plate."

"Well, dad." She starts, abruptly. "That's because I'm grateful for what I have. I make sure to cherish every single meal I get to enjoy in my life," She looks back at me. "Because you never know when it could be taken away, right Marcus?" A menacing scowl takes over her face and I can feel the tension mounting. Very funny.

"Unfortunately, life isn't fair." I respond with a phoney empathetic look. The room falls silent and Sky's family can almost certainly feel our tension.

Our discreet conversation of digs continues throughout the lunch. Every word we exchange is laced with underlying meaning, a game of cat and mouse that neither of us seems willing to back down from. As the lunch comes to a close, Sky's mother begins to clear the dishes, her eyes darting between us with a mix of suspicion and concern. I can see the wheels turning in her head, trying to decipher the meaning behind our cryptic conversation. She stands up with a small stack of plates.

"Right then," She starts with a smile, "I think it's time for some birthday cake. Marcus, darling, will you come and help me?"

"Of course." I respond, grabbing the rest of the plates on my way.

Sky's mother hands me an old tin full of various, mismatched candles and some matches. I begin placing them around the cake in a strategic pattern, making sure that they're evenly spaced. Some are tall and slender, with long, thin wicks that curl and twist as they burn. Others are short and stout, with thicker wicks. I strike the matches and hold them to the candles, watching as their flames leap up eagerly, casting a warm glow over the room. The scent of burning wax filling my nose, reminding me of childhood birthdays. That's pretty much all we had back at Orchid's. A birthday cake and a gift under £20.

As I step back to admire my handiwork, Sky's mother gasps happily, as if my mediocre candle placement is a work of art.

"Beautiful! Thank you for the help."

"Of course."

She scurries off excitedly to switch off the living room light and returns quickly to begin carrying the cake. As she begins to lift the cake, my attention diverts momentarily to the drawer tucked beneath her. I attempt to hide my creeping, impish smile with my hand, barely able to contain the playful anticipation bubbling within me, as I wait for her to begin walking away. *Let's see if Sky has a snarky remark to make about this.* With a flick of my wrist I grab the knife from the drawer and slip it into my back pocket, before following her lead.

We begin singing in unison.

'Happy birthday to you...happy birthday to you...'

I lock onto Sky with an icy glare. Anger still painted across her face. As we reach the second line of the song, I reach into my back pocket and pull out the knife, twiddling it idly between my fingers. The dim candle light glinting ominously on its surface. A brief moment passes before realisation of my intent dawns on her. Her mouth snaps shut, and the vibrant red hue of her face swiftly drains to a pallid white. The tension in the room is now thick enough to cut with the very knife I'm wielding. As the chorus fills the air, the innocence of the song clashes violently with the dark, twisted dance between her and I. Her chest heaving as she struggles to maintain her composure.

I twirl the knife deftly, a sinister ballet in my fingertips. The movement is deliberate, a silent taunt that only she and I understand. The singing morphs into a haunting symphony in my mind, each note a discordant echo amplifying the silent turmoil between us. It's as if the very air around us is charged with our unspoken confrontation. Sky's facade crumbles slowly. Her attempt at maintaining composure battles against the fear that's etched across her face. Her eyes dart between mine and the knife, an unspoken dialogue of terror and defiance. I hold her gaze, revelling in the fear that courses through her veins. The power shift between us is palpable, a thrilling rush that electrifies the charged atmosphere.

The blade dances on, a macabre conductor orchestrating the sinister duet we perform. The song finally comes to a close, the last note hanging in the air like a lingering echo of the turmoil that just transpired. Sky's breaths are ragged, her facade barely holding up against the sheer weight of our unspoken confrontation. I meet her gaze one last time, a silent promise of more to come, before turning away and seamlessly joining the applause for the birthday boy as he blows out the candles, my expression a mask of casual indifference.

As the chatter and laughter crescendo, I take a step toward the table where the birthday cake awaits, an innocent smile playing on my lips.

"Who wants the first slice?" I announce cheerfully, my voice cutting through the jovial atmosphere. Sky's eyes widen with a mixture of dread and disbelief as she watches me approach the cake, her unease blatant.

"Sky?" I offer with a deceptive charm, my tone laced with an undercurrent of menace that only she can detect. Her breath catches in her throat, her eyes fixated on the glinting blade. A sudden wave of obvious nausea washes over her.

"I-I'm fine, thanks." She manages to stutter. Ignoring her refusal, I move closer, the knife glinting under the ambient light. The room seems to hold its breath, the festive air tainted by an unspoken tension. I begin to slice. And slice again. The piece falling softly from the knife and onto the paper plate. I extend my hand towards her and place the plate at her fingertips.

Sky's face fills with pure disgust.

"Sky, are you alright, darling?" Her mother questions. Without a word, she pushes back from the table, the chair scraping against the floor in her haste. She staggers to her feet, her hand clasped over her mouth as she rushes out of the room, a torrent of emotions evident in her hurried departure. The room falls into an uncomfortable silence, the cheerful ambiance shattered by her abrupt exit. Murmurs of concern and confusion ripple through her family, but I maintain a facade of nonchalance, carefully concealing the thrill that pulses beneath the surface.

With a casual shrug, I set the knife down beside the cake, effortlessly blending back into the facade of normalcy.

"Guess she's not feeling well," I remark, my voice carrying an air of faux concern. The room attempts to return to its previous state of celebration, but an unspoken tension lingers, a reminder of the chilling exchange that just unfolded. I continue to play my part, engaging in small talk and laughter, effortlessly slipping back into the role of the affable guest. But beneath the facade, a sense of exhilaration thrums within me, a rush fueled by the power I wielded in that fleeting moment.

Checkmate.

CHAPTER 24:

BIKER'S DELIGHT

I lightly knock on the front door, the sound echoing faintly in the hallway, while I patiently await Delilah's answer. She soon greets me in the doorway, her hair messy and exhaustion written all over her tiny face. She barely mutters a word and walks straight into the living room. Closing the front door I plod in behind her, the echo of my entry lost in the palpable fatigue that hangs heavy in the air. My friends, usually high and bubbly, are instead worn-out and worn-down. Scattered around like fallen soldiers in a battle they never signed up for. Dean, our unfortunate general, looks like he's gone ten rounds with a tornado and lost.

"Where's Skylar?" Birdie asks.

"She wasn't feeling too good." I respond, taking a seat on the arm of the sofa.

"Join the club." Dean snaps, rightfully so.

"Why didn't you stay in the hospital?"

"If I'm gonna die, I'm not dying in a hospital." He states; I can see the fury and impatience building up inside him.

The room seems to hold its breath, each of us lost in our thoughts, silently grappling with the weight of the situation. The fatigue is a tangible entity, wrapping itself around us like a heavy shroud. Delilah sinks into the armchair, exhaustion etched into every line on her face.

"Any progress?" she asks, her voice barely audible.

"A little," I respond, almost scared of the building reaction to whatever will come out of my mouth. "I went to see Millie." The room once again falls into a silence at my revelation. It's as if I've dropped a bombshell, one that no one expected, especially considering our collective uncertainty towards Millie. I can feel their eyes on me, questioning and confused. Dean's brow furrows in disbelief.

"Why the fuck would you wanna go and talk to that snob?"

"You think she has something to do with all of this?" Delilah asks.

"She's the answer to all of this, I'm sure of it. We can't close the book without her."

"Are you sure?" Birdie questions, "We haven't heard from her in years." At this point I can feel the scepticism in the room cutting into my flesh.

"I know, but unfortunately for us she's the queen in the story." All of their doubt is weighing down on me and I feel as though I'm disappointing them more and more with every word leaving my lips.

"Well, what did she say?" Delilah asks with concern. I take a sharp breath before answering honestly.

"She was pretty pissed and uh, she basically told me to get out."

Fuck I wish the ground would just swallow me.

"Well that's fantastic. I'm *so* glad to hear that my life is in her hands." Dean says, now standing agitatedly.

"I get it, I get it." I try to reassure, rubbing my face with my hands. "You guys just have to trust me."

"Incase you haven't noticed, I'm running out of time here. I'm sick and tired of sitting around and talking about this bullshit." He states, shaking his head, "Get the book out right now and we'll glue the fucker shut." I can sense the room's temperature dropping as Dean's frustration soars to new heights. His demand for the book making my heart pound a little faster. Their anger is warranted, but what I have to reveal might just push them over the edge.

"I don't have it." I mumble. I look into Dean's eyes and can see he's about to explode. *If he was feeling better I'd likely have a fist in my face right about now.*

"You what?" He asks. I don't repeat myself. He doesn't actually want me to. Instead I swallow hard, the weight of his glare suffocating. I can practically feel the heat radiating from him. I know he feels like I'm letting him down, but I know what I'm doing. I know his words are fueled by fear, by desperation. The weight of his expectations bears down on me, each syllable heavy with disappointment and anger. A raw intensity flickers in Dean's eyes.

"What do you mean you don't have it?" His voice rises, the anger simmering beneath the surface.

"I left it with Millie."

"You're a fucking idiot."

"She needs to read it." I assert, holding onto my certainty that this is the only way forward, even if it feels like I'm standing against a hurricane.

"You have no idea what she's gonna do with that book." Dean counters, his voice a tumultuous clash echoing off the walls.

"She'll read it, man. Trust me. I've got this."

"You're full of shit."

"I know what I'm doing."

"We can't afford to take those kinds of risks." Delilah interrupts.

"We don't have a choice. We can't do this without her." I reiterate. With that, Sienna readjusts her seating position with a frustrated sigh.

"Oh my God, Marcus. We get it. *Queen Millie's gonna save the day, blah blah blah.*"

Damn, there's my angry little sweet.

Her hostility at my mention of Millie is stirring a mix of emotions inside of me. It's a nice change to see my Sienna getting a little possessive, but I'll have to make sure she learns quickly that talking to me like that is going to get her in trouble.

"I'm very sorry, sweet." I say with a smirk. Sienna's crossed arms and narrowed eyes tell me she's not having any of it. I get it; she's protective, and bringing up Millie might have struck a nerve.

That's okay, I'll make it up to her.

Dean walks up closer to me, his stance is angry but I can tell from his eyes he's pleading.

"Do me a favour, fuck off and go get the book back."

I look around the room in search of some support, which of course doesn't come.

"Fine."

I walk out, leaving the heat and tension behind me, the front door closing with a firm thud. The warm night air outside is a welcomed relief, a balm to my frayed nerves. I make my way out of the front garden and lean against the brick wall in wait of my sweet Sienna, who I know will be foolishly assuming she can make her way home alone. Watching the stars speckling the sky is a peaceful contrast to the chaos inside. I reach for a cigarette, but the allure of a joint tucked in my pocket calls to me instead. A sigh escapes as I light it, the flame casting fleeting shadows that dance around my form. A sense of calmness settles within me, amplified by the soft rustling of the leaves in the gentle breeze. Minutes pass, marked by the rhythmic puffs of smoke that dissipate into the velvety night.

As I hear the door opening I crush the spent joint against the ground. The soft shuffle of steps approaches, and in the dimly lit night, Birdie and Sienna emerge, their attempt to disregard me palpable as they stride toward the front gate. Without hesitation, I reach out, seizing Sienna's wrist in a firm grip, halting her retreat. The subtle resistance she offers does nothing to deter my determined pull, drawing her back into my orbit. I wait for Birdie to walk away before turning to face Sienna with a stern scowl.

"Where do you think you're going?"

"Home." She replies sarcastically.

"On your own? Not happening." I state firmly, my tone leaving no room for negotiation.

"I can handle myself."

"I'm sure you can, but I'm not willing to test it out."

"You're not my boyfriend, Marcus." she snaps. I laugh.

"You may not be my girlfriend, *Sienna*, but you are mine. In every sense of the word," I sneer. She tugs feebly at her hand, 'attempting' to free herself from my grip, but I don't let go. Instead, I take a step closer, our bodies almost touching, and lower my voice to a whisper. "You think I'm just going to let you walk away from me like that?" I challenge, my eyes locked with hers.

Holy fuck, she's so beautiful.

"What do you want?" She sighs.

"Right now, I want you to show me some respect," I start, "Or this attitude is going to get you into trouble." She tries to maintain her defiance, but her voice wavers slightly as she responds,

"I don't appreciate being treated like a possession."

"It's not possession, sweet. It's an addiction." A shiver runs down her spine, and I can see the internal battle raging within her. The desire to resist, to maintain control, warms with her desperate need to surrender. With a final surge of determination, she pushes me away, her hands finding their way to my chest.

"I won't be controlled, Marcus," she says, her voice steady, but her eyes smouldering with a fiery intensity. I chuckle softly, the challenge in her eyes only fueling my desire.

"Who said anything about control? I don't want to control you, sweet. I want to worship you. To explore every inch of your body until you're begging me for release. I want to give you pleasure like you've never experienced before."

With a newfound hunger, I press my lips against hers, claiming her in a searing kiss. Our bodies meld together, each touch and caress a testament to our shared need, our shared addiction. Her resistance falters further, a breathless sigh escaping her lips. I take the opportunity to press my body against hers, allowing her to feel the undeniable evidence of my own yearning. The tension between us crackles in the air, the world fading away until it's just the two of us once again, caught in a web of desire and power.

Sienna's eyes flutter closed, surrendering to the intoxicating pull we share. I release her wrists, my hands now free to roam over her body, memorising every curve and dip. I pause to whisper in her ear.

"You think you can resist me, but I can feel how your body betrays you, how your pulse quickens beneath my touch." I say, my voice dripping with smug satisfaction. "I killed for you and you still have no idea what I'm capable of. If you want to be disobedient, my sweet, I can make you forget your own name. You'll forget every reason why you tried to fight me in the first place." Sienna's lips part, a soft whimper escaping as my thumb brushes against her inner thigh, edging closer to the heat between her legs. Her eyes darken with a mix of anticipation and surrender.

In one smooth motion, I sweep my 5-foot-nothing angel off her feet and carry her over to my motorbike, sitting her sideways on the seat, my body still pressed against hers.

"Marcus, what are you doin-" she says softly.

"Open." I command. She doesn't respond, and instead meets me with a bewildered look.

"Your legs, sweet. Open your legs." She hesitates for a moment, a beautiful hint of fear in her eyes, but begins slowly parting her legs. *Too slow for my liking*. I grip her thighs and forcefully spread her legs open, exposing her further.

Without wasting another second, I keep one hand tightly holding open her thigh and begin tracing underneath her skirt with the other. My fingers reach her underwear and slowly hook into them, shifting them to the side; remaining eye contact. Teasing her entrance with a featherlight touch. Her face flustered. Sienna's breath hitches, her eyes widening with a mix of excitement and vulnerability. The thrill of the forbidden fills the air as I continue to touch her, my movements deliberate and calculated. I run a finger upwards and stop once I reach her clit, pulsing it lightly. She begins to whimper and her arms reach down to grab my hand. I hold her arms firmly, refusing to let her take control of the situation.

"No, sweet. You're not allowed to touch," I growl, my voice laced with authority. Sienna's eyes widen even more, a delicious mix of arousal and uncertainty swimming within them. I can feel her body trembling beneath my touch, the anticipation building with each passing second. Without warning, I slide a finger inside her, feeling her wetness coating me. She gasps, her back arching involuntarily against the bike. I move my finger slowly, teasingly, relishing in the way her breath becomes ragged as her pleasure intensifies.

She becomes more flustered and begins looking to her side, afraid of being caught. I firmly grab her chin and turn her back to face me.

"Eyes on me, Sienna."

Her gasps turn into whimpers as I find her sweet spot, my fingers skillfully working their magic.

"*Fuck,* you're so tight." I smirk at her moans of pleasure and decide to push her further. With a devilish glint in my eyes, I add another finger, stretching her slightly to accommodate the new sensation. Sienna's eyes widen in surprise as I continue to pump my fingers inside her, matching the rhythm of her moans. Each stroke sends waves of pleasure coursing through her body, her grip on the bike tightening. I lean in closer, kissing and nibbling at her neck as I whisper,

"You like that, don't you, sweet?" She can only nod, her words lost in a whirlwind of pleasure and desire. My fingers explore her folds, parting them gently to delve deeper. She continues to moan softly, her hips instinctively shifting against my hand, seeking more contact. "You look so pretty like this."

I pick up the pace, my fingers dancing over her sensitive clit, applying just the right amount of pressure to drive her wild. Sienna's moans grow louder, her breathing ragged. Her hands now gripping deep into the seat of the bike. I can feel her walls contracting around my fingers, a sign that she's getting closer to the edge.

But just as she's about to tip over into ecstasy, I withdraw my fingers, leaving her panting and unsatisfied. Her eyes shoot open, a mixture of confusion and frustration in her gaze. I give her an indulgent smile, knowing exactly what I'm doing to her.

"Did you think it would be that easy, sweet?" I tease, my voice dripping with lust. I lean back and take in the sight before me. Sienna, flushed and panting, her eyes filled with a mixture of anticipation and frustration, aching for the pleasure I can provide. My hold on her thighs tightens, another silent reminder of my control.

"Now, sweet, I want to hear you beg for me." I demand.

I eagerly await her response, my gaze locked on her tight. The silence that follows is heavy with tension, each passing second amplifying the anticipation in the air. Her chest rises and falls rapidly, her lips trembling as she tries to find the right words. Finally, she takes a deep breath, her voice quivering as she speaks.

"Marcus-"

"Beg."

"Please," she whispers, her voice filled with need. A wicked grin spreads across my face, an intoxicating combination of triumph and desire. My thumb caresses her inner thigh, the touch light yet tantalising, as I lean in closer to her ear.

"Good girl," I growl, my breath hot against her skin. I reach between her legs once again, my fingers eagerly finding their way inside of her. This time, I don't hold back. I delve deep into her, my fingers moving with a hunger that matches her own. The sound of her moans fills the night air, mingling with the soft rustle of leaves and the distant hum of passing cars.

As I pleasure her, I study her every reaction, taking note of what drives her wild. I devour her gasps and moans, savouring the taste of her pleasure mingling with the night. With each stroke and curl of my fingers, I can feel her walls tightening around me, her body teetering on the edge of release. I lovingly stroke her cheek, the cruel smirk on my face contrasting with the tenderness in my touch.

"I want to hear you beg a little more."

Sienna's eyes lock with mine, her desire burning brighter than ever. With a pleading look, she whispers,

"Please,"

"Please?" I raise an eyebrow at her.

"Please let me come."

The desperation in her voice is like music to my ears. It fuels my arousal, making me more determined to push her to her limits. My fingers return to her core, expertly working their magic. I alternate between gentle caresses and firm strokes, bringing her closer and closer to the edge with each passing moment.

Her moans become louder, she's on the precipice of climax, her muscles tensing as she fights against the overwhelming pleasure coursing through her veins. Sensing her imminent release, I lean in close, my lips grazing her ear.

"There you go," I whisper. With those words, Sienna's resistance shatters. Her body convulses with euphoria as her orgasm crashes over her, wave after wave of pleasure coursing through her body. I release Sienna from my grip, allowing her to recover from the intense pleasure that just washed over her. As her breathing slows and her body relaxes, I lean in closer.

"Now I get to taste you, right sweet?"
Without waiting for a response, I crouch down in front of her, my hands still firmly gripping her thighs. her eyes widen with a mix of shock and anticipation as she realises what I have in mind. The crisp night air adds an extra thrill to the moment as I slide her skirt up, revealing her pussy. Seeing it for the first time feels indescribably rewarding.

I bury my face between her legs, inhaling her intoxicating sweet scent before flicking my tongue lightly against her clit. She gasps, her hands instinctively reaching for my hair, but I grab her wrists and pull them away, maintaining control. I want to show her that this pleasure is all about me, that she is at my mercy. I continue to tease her, alternating between gentle licks and firm sucks, relishing in the way her moans grow louder and her hips instinctively grind against my mouth. The taste of her arousal is addictive, driving me to explore every inch of her with my tongue.

With each flick and swirl of my tongue, her body trembles, her pleasure building with a ferocious intensity. She tugs and scratches at the seat, craving the release that only I can give her. I tighten my grip on her thighs, holding her firmly in place, denying her the freedom she so desperately seeks.

As I continue to devour her, my own arousal intensifies, evident by the bulge pressing against my tracksuit bottoms. I release one of my hands from her thigh, reaching down to free my erect length from its confines and returning my hand instantly. My body aches with the desperate need for release; the craving to bend her over this bike and fuck her from behind. To fill her and watch her drip. But I resist the urge to give in to my own desires. Right now, it's all about Sienna. I focus solely on giving her pleasure, my tongue working fervently against her sensitive bundle of nerves. Her moans grow louder, more desperate, as I bring her closer to the edge once again. The vibration of her pleas sends shivers down my spine, and I can feel myself throbbing with need. But I remind myself to stay patient, to savour this moment of control.

Her body tenses beneath me, her breathing becoming erratic as she nears her second climax. I can sense it, the way her muscles tighten, the way her hips grind against my mouth. She's on the precipice, just a few more flicks of my tongue and she will fall into bliss. With one final lick, my tongue flat, I push her over the edge, her body convulsing as waves of pleasure crash over her.

I continue to lap up her sweet essence, savouring every drop as she rides out her orgasm. The taste of her on my tongue is intoxicating, driving me to a new level of insanity. As her moans fade into soft gasps of satisfaction, I place a kiss on her swollen clit and release her thighs before standing back up to look down at her flushed and needy state. I chuckle softly, relishing in the power I hold over her. I lean in close, my lips brushing against her ear as I ask,

"You want me to fuck you, sweet? You want me to prove that you're mine?" She nods, her breathing rapid and shallow. "Then beg for it. Beg me to fuck you."

"Please-" I grab her throat, tight enough that she should be seeing some stars, and force her to look deep into my eyes. *She fucking smiles. Holy shit.*

"Please, what? Tell me what I want to hear."

"Fuck me." *This can't be real. Is this real? I hope so.*

"Who do you belong to?" I ask.

She hesitates for a moment and attempts to gulp through her restricted throat.

"You."

I smirk proudly and shake my head.

"I'm not gonna fuck you yet." I step back, a triumphant smile on my face as I deny her request. She looks up at me confused. "Not tonight. I want to take my time with you." She attempts to hide the smile creeping onto her face by sucking in her bottom lip. I crouch down to her eye level and brush my hand across her cheek. "I've got you for life, Sienna. I don't wanna rush a single thing." I kiss her forehead and stand back up straight, my eyes not leaving hers.

"Come on, sweet. Let's get you home."

CHAPTER 25:
TRY AGAIN

11:00 a.m. Back to apartment No.2 I go. I ring the buzzer. No need to lie about who I am this time. Millie's rapid response to let me in surprises me, almost as though she's been anticipating my arrival. That can't be good. I reach the top of the stairs and I'm immediately met by Millie's viscous gaze as she stands in the doorway, book in hand. Neither of us speak, and the absence of words feels unsettling, amplifying the strained atmosphere that suffuses the space.

Little bit awkward, Millie.

Millie remains steadfast, her silence cutting deeper than any words could. Instead, she slowly extends the book towards me, a deliberate movement. I accept the book with a hesitant nod, meeting Millie's unyielding gaze. The exchange lingers. It's not often people make me feel uncomfortable, but she's an enigmatic figure.

"So uh, did you read it?" I manage to force out, a feeble attempt to ease the observable discomfort. A beat passes, the air laden with anticipation, until, unexpectedly, Millie's response is stark and unembellished.

"Yes." The simplicity of her reply in the midst of this surreal moment strikes a chord that teeters on the edge of comical and absurd. In the midst of this bizarre exchange, I can't help but stifle a nervous chuckle, the tension momentarily broken by the sheer peculiarity of it all. Millie's stern expression doesn't waver.

"So what are you thinking?" I venture cautiously, hoping to prod some rationale from the enigma that is Millie Devons.

"The answer is no." Her reply, devoid of any embellishment or explanation, cuts through the tension like a blade. The abruptness of her refusal stuns me momentarily. The absurdity of the situation, coupled with the gravity of what's at stake, threatens to tip the scales between irritation and amusement.

"You can't seriously be that childish."

"You claim to have brought me a magical book, and *I'm* childish?" She scoffs. Millie's retort hits a nerve, her sarcasm twisting the situation into an absurd tangle of frustration and disbelief. I chuckle slightly in anger.

"You're impossible. Dean's life is on the line and you're acting like this?" The exasperation in my voice is tangible, a mixture of anger and desperation bubbling beneath the surface.

"Go ask Sienna for help."

This fucking bitch.

The mere mention of Sienna's name from her pretentious mouth is like a lit match in a room drenched in gasoline.

"How dare you even say her name."

"Does she know that I'm the queen in your little book?" Millie's spiteful words cut through the air, a venomous arrow aimed at distorting reality. I scoff at the absurdity of her claim. The audacity of her implication catches me off guard, the insinuation so far from the truth that it's almost laughable.

"You're nothing to me-"

"There's always a hint of truth in story books," she interrupts, her words dripping with condescension. I can't help but laugh out loud.

"Millie. You're the queen in the book because 11 year old me was in his feelings over the fact that Sienna didn't want me." She has the audacity to look hurt. So I continue, "I would wipe you off the face of the earth in a heartbeat for her. Is that clear?"

"You're really still that obsessed with her after all these years?"

"You seem pretty obsessed with her yourself." I counter. Millie's face contorts with anger and frustration.

"I don't care about Sienna." She hisses.

"You've always been jealous of Sienna, ever since we were kids, that's why you fucking picked on her."

She rolls her eyes and cackles spitefully which sends me into a frenzy.

"Oh please, I never picked on her. I went through hell in that home. You have no idea what you're talking abou-"

"I'm not doing this, Millie." I interrupt, shaking my head. "I didn't come here to listen to your shitty little sob stories. This is about Dean." Millie's face softens momentarily, a flicker of concern crossing her features before returning to her usual stoic expression. She says nothing and I allow the silence to linger for a moment, hoping it will cool things down.

"Is he in a bad way?" She finally mumbles, a sliver of humanity actually peeking through. Images of Dean's wilting face from last night flash into my mind. I feel a lump form in my throat, swallowing hard before responding.

"Yeah." My voice cracks slightly as I speak through the emotions. "And he's just getting worse." Each word seems to carve a deeper groove of concern into my heart, mirroring the gravity of Dean's deteriorating state. The weight of Dean's condition finally seems to be reaching Millie. Her gaze falls to the book in my hands, a hint of guilt shadowing her features. The tension in the room shifts as a shared concern for Dean's well-being seems to unite us briefly.

"Did you read the last line of the book carefully, Marcus?" I look at her in a confused scowl.

"Close the gates." I quote.

"To protect the village." She counters. "You haven't stopped to think about the fact that Dean is the villain in this story? A threat to the rest of us. The village." I stop to think about her words, goosebumps running up my arms. I shake the suggestion away and bring myself back to my goal.

"It's a possibility," I admit, "But it's a risk I'm willing to take. He's my brother, Millie, and I need him alive. Villain or not."

As her eyes meet mine again, a rare glimpse of genuine emotion flickers within them, softening the edges of her guarded demeanour.

"I'm sorry," She murmurs, shaking her head. "I have to go." Before I can process her words, she starts to retreat, backing away into her apartment. Confusion and frustration surge within me, an urgent plea rising in my throat.

"Wait." I quickly jam my foot in the crack of the door and look intensely at her. One last attempt, Marcus.

"Look, I don't care what you think about me. This isn't about us. Millie, If Dean doesn't make it, his blood is on your hands. You can't just walk away from this."

I remove my foot and stand back, hoping for a response. Instead, the door inches closed, the barrier between hope and hopelessness now shut. The definitive click of the door echoing through my ears. I stand alone in the corridor, the book in my hand feeling heavier than before. A knot of despair constricts my chest, every breath a struggle against the invisible shackles of powerlessness. Tears well up, a silent testament to the maelstrom of emotions raging within, but they refuse to spill, trapped behind a dam of frustration and anguish. The knowledge that Dean's lifeline may have just slipped away leaves me hollow, my spirit crumbling under the weight of my inadequacy.

Dean's gaunt face, etched with suffering, haunts my thoughts, each fading memory another lash upon my soul. The weight of responsibility presses down, heavier than I've ever known, the realisation that I failed to secure the help Dean so desperately needs clawing at my conscience. But there's nothing more I can do. I can do nothing but wait, and hope.

The short journey to my bike feels like a trail through a desolate wasteland. Each step is heavy, burdened not just by the physical weight of my body but by the weight of my failure. I can't shake the exhaustion settling in, not just from the encounter but from the entirety of this futile quest for help. It's like shouting into a void and receiving only echoes in return. I'm fed up with this relentless cycle of trying and failing, and each step back to my bike adds another layer of disillusionment.

I slide my hand into my pocket to grab my bike key. The familiar cool metal meeting my fingertips, grounding me in a reality I'm not entirely ready to confront. A long, weary sigh escapes my lips, a mix of frustration and resignation. It's as if I can taste their metallic tang against my tongue as I pull them out.

With a jaded flick of my wrist, I insert the key into the ignition, the soft click ironically signalling readiness. The engine's growl is a comforting reminder in a world that feels increasingly foreign. With a subtle nudge, I shift the bike into gear, feeling the subtle resistance beneath my boot. My bike hums in anticipation, a faithful steed awaiting its rider's command.

The wind greets me, ruffling my clothes and tousling my hair, as if encouraging me to leave everything behind. The weight of responsibility, the day's stresses, they all begin to fade into my mirrors. Each bend in the road demands my attention, and I respond, leaning into the curves with a fluidity that comes from years of riding. There's a rhythm to the ride, a synergy between man and machine that's more than just a dance; it's an understanding, an unspoken language where the bike becomes an extension of my being.

For me, riding isn't just a hobby. It's a way of life, a passion that courses through my veins. The ride becomes more than a means of transport; it's a sanctuary where I find solace, rejuvenation, and a sense of belonging. And I need all of the above right now.

CHAPTER 26:

BOOK MAIL

I coast along the urban arteries, the wind weaving through my hair. Stopped in traffic, my eye is suddenly drawn to the bookstore across the street. Sienna loves going there. It's then that I remember that I had taken a sneaky picture of her book wishlist she'd scribbled down a few weeks ago. Maybe today, amidst the chaos, grabbing my sweet some gifts could be my flicker of light.

After all, she was a very good girl for me last night.

I pull up outside the shop entrance, enjoying a cigarette as I dig through my phone for the image.

It doesn't take long to locate the list since I don't have much saved on my phone. Just sneaky pictures I had taken of my beautiful Sienna and a shitload of bike videos. There are eleven books on the list. Easy. With the image in hand, I flick the cigarette to the ground and pocket my phone. Stepping into the store, the familiar scent of paper and ink envelops me. It's actually a comforting embrace amid the city's hustle. My gaze sweeps the shelves, scanning titles and sections.

I'm fumbling through this place, surrounded by rows upon rows of books that might as well be written in some ancient language. Sienna's wishlist, the crumpled photo on my shattered phone screen, is my only guide in this sea of words and covers. Classics, poetry, fiction, non-fiction, authors I've never heard of; my knowledge barely scratches the surface. Sienna deserves more than my cluelessness, but fuck, I'm trying. I clutch the list, scanning titles as if I might just magically stumble upon exactly what she wants.

In the end, I admit defeat. I approach the cashier, pulling out my phone with her scrawled wishlist.

"Hey, just wondering if you could help me find these books." With a mix of resignation and hope, I hand it over, silently pleading for assistance. She grabs the phone and begins reading the list, a smile creeping on her face.

"So you're a romance book kinda-guy, huh?" She says playfully.

"They're not for me." I clarify, rubbing my neck.

"Yeah, that's what they all say. Follow me." she beckons, leading the way. Her willingness to assist turns this daunting task into a delightful adventure. Together, we navigate the shelves, her expertise guiding me through the literary cosmos to find the treasures on Sienna's list. With each book found, I can't help but feel a surge of gratitude toward this stranger aiding me on my quest to spoil my angel.

She stops at one book on the list,

"This one is part of a series, are you looking for just the one or the whole set?" she asks. Leisurely I reply,

"If you have the whole series that'd be great."

Would it, Marcus? What if she has the rest of the set already?

As we continue searching I stop to look at the size of the mounting pile of books in our hands and I can't help but wonder about the expanding hole in my wallet. Books aren't that expensive, right? I continue to glance at them in an attempt to mentally calculate just how much this random adventure is going to cost me. After what feels like hours, it seems this treasure hunt is nearing its end. The cashier glances at our increasingly hefty bundle of books and chuckles softly.

"That's a full house, what a lucky girl." she says, gleaming.

But Sienna isn't lucky. This is nothing. She deserves the world.

The cashier scans each book, the beeps marking the countdown of my recklessness. With every beep, I'm watching the total add up on the screen. It's more than I anticipated. A lot more.

"That'll be £178.84"

Nearly £200 on books. Have I lost my mind? I stand there, and my mind drifts back to the countless mornings I've spent on construction sites for some extra cash. The backbreaking labour, the sweat, and the occasional cursing at a stubborn nail or an uncooperative piece of wood, surrounded by loudmouths I can't stand. Things like this are what it's all for. Hearing Sienna's laughter, watching her eyes light up when she talks about her favourite stories. That's what I'm working for.

Your money is there to spoil Sienna with, Marcus.

I grit my teeth and hand over my card, plastering a smile on my face that I hope looks confident and unfazed by the cost. The cashier hands back my card along with a mighty stack of books wrapped in a store-branded bag, giving me a knowing nod as if she understands my plight.

I make my way onto Sienna's doorstep, holding the bag of books I had carefully picked for her. My heartbeat seems to synchronise with the knocking rhythm. A second passes, and then the door creaks open, revealing Sienna's adorable curious face.

"What are you doing here?" she asks, trying to hide her pretty little smile. I hold out the bag of books for her to take. "What's that?" I nod down at the bag slightly as a gesture for her to take it.

"I bought you some gifts." I say, a faint smile tugging at the corners of my lips. She looks at me in awe and attempts to grab the bag, the weight of it pulling her arms down.

"Marcus, you didn't have to-"

"You deserve it, sweet." She vaguely rummages through the bag, her fingers tracing the book spines. Her doe eyes alighting with delight as she recognizes familiar titles among the mix. A grateful smile brightens her face, and for a moment, the air feels lighter, as if the tension I carried in my chest has dissolved.

"How did you know which books to get?" she asks, bewildered.

"That's for me to know." I tease. We pause momentarily, soaking up each other's eye contact and grinning from ear to ear.

Fuck I'm so in love.

"What have you been up to today then?" I ask, rolling up a blunt in the meantime.

"I went on a date." She jokes bravely.

"Oh yeah?" I raise an eyebrow, feigning surprise. "Who do I have to kill this time?" I ask with a devilish grin. Utter shock takes over her face for a brief moment, as if she had forgotten my heinous act, committed in her honour. She swallows her shock and smiles timidly.

"He was very charming. He bought me a bag of books."

Nice recovery, sweet.

"Ah, now he sounds like a real catch." I wink, finishing up the blunt and lighting it. The pungent scent fills the cool air, and I'm momentarily lost in the familiar ritual. Sienna's expression shifts, her amusement replaced with a much more serious look.

"Marcus, you know that stuff isn't good for you, right?" I exhale a plume of smoke, considering her question.

"And going on dates with men who wear skinny jeans is any better?" I challenge. Sienna sighs, shaking her head. "It helps me unwind, sweet." She crosses her arms, her gaze unyielding.

"There are better ways to unwind, Marcus. Healthier ways." I chuckle.

"You sound like my conscience." Her eyes soften as she regards me, a subtle understanding passing between us.

"You need a new hobby. Something that won't slowly kill you." I smile and nod slowly.

"I'll think about it."

"Not good enough." She remains locked in her grumpy face, her arms firmly crossed, so I crouch down to her eye level. I take another drag and turn my head to the side to exhale away from her face.

"Sweet, if you're gonna be naughty, I'll take those books back and give you something else instead." I threaten playfully, raising my eyebrows. Her beautiful big eyes widen and I watch her pupils dilate. With that I place a kiss on her forehead and stand back up straight. She sucks in her bottom lip and starts backing into the entryway.

"Thank you for the books." She says softly.

"You're welcome, sweet. I'll see you soon."

CHAPTER 27:

FUGITIVE FRIENDS

7:20p.m. Getting back after a long joy ride, I lie down on my bed, permitting my mind to be clear for a change. This room has definitely become a small haven for me, an oasis from the storm of obligations outside.

As usual, my peace is destroyed rather quickly.

The door slams open, hitting the wall behind, and Skylar charges in; her voice a tempest in the calm. I had been successful at avoiding her after the birthday lunch but clearly there's no option now. Her eyes pierce through me, harbouring an anger I recognize too well. But she started it. How could I resist? Knowing her hands were tied, locked in a vault with my darkest secret.

"You feeling better?" I dare to ask, an arrogant smile breaking out.

"Fuck you, Marcus! What the hell was that all about?" Her words seethe with indignation, her eyes ablaze.

"Just a bit of banter, Sky. Relax." I say, my tone far too casual, trying to dismiss the gravity of my actions.

"Banter?" Her voice begins to rise in an ear-splitting screech. It's like nails on a chalkboard.

"You can't tell me you didn't find it a little funny. And anyway, you started it."

"Funny? Marcus, this is serious." I adjust my pillow, unfazed.

"What's done is done, Sky. You pushed me to tell you my little secret and so now you're as trapped as I am. Get over it," Skylar's frustration intensifies at my dismissive attitude. She paces the room, her anger tangible.

"Do you even care? I mean, I didn't even kill anybody and yet this whole thing is eating me alive. But you're so, so-" She pauses and looks at me, flustered and struggling to find any words. I vaguely lift my head off my pillow and look back at her, expressionless. "So calm."

"What do you want me to do, Sky? Curl up in a ball and cry? Pace back and forth like a lunatic? Because that *really* seems to be working for you."

"Do you not feel anything? Any remorse?" She questions.

"Look, you've got your own way of dealing with things. I've got mine. Can you leave me alone now?"

With that, she shakes her head and leaves, slamming the door on the way out of course. In the midst of this chaos, an unexpected calmness once again descends, a rare occurrence that leaves me bewildered. Relaxation is a foreign notion to an insomniac like me, yet an unexplained tranquillity invites me to succumb to sleep.

Am I actually about to have a nap?

The concept is alien to me. As my eyelids yield to the weight, the world fades into the distance, and I surrender to the rare allure. Sleep envelopes me, and there are no vivid dreams, no surreal landscapes, just a void. A vacuum. My mind simply floating in an empty expanse of darkness. It's a peculiar sensation, devoid of the usual rush of thoughts and images that frequent my mind. This absence of dreams feels almost deafening in its silence. No subconscious narratives or fragmented whispers traversing my slumbering mind. No fantasies of having my way with Sienna. Literally nothing but blackness. It's as if time has paused, leaving me adrift in an abyss of nothingness, disconnected from the usual currents of consciousness.

As moments pass, though in the realm of sleep, time feels elusive. I hover on the edge of awareness, suspended in a state of rest that feels both unfamiliar and oddly serene. A strange comfort within the void.

Eventually, consciousness tiptoes back, gently nudging me from the abyss of dreamless sleep. I emerge, somewhat disoriented yet strangely refreshed, as if the emptiness within had briefly found solace in the absence of thoughts. Opening my eyes, I find the room unchanged, the echoes of the confrontation with Skylar lingering in the air. My fingers stretch out, navigating through the sheets to reach my phone. As the screen illuminates at my touch, revealing the time in its glowing digits, I notice a map etched upon my arm in the form of deep sleep lines, like delicate rivers marking their way along the terrain of my skin. I can't even remember the last time I had them. The significance of these imprints looms large, an enigmatic reminder of a sleep so peaceful it feels almost mythical. The memory of such undisturbed repose feels elusive, distant; like an echo from a forgotten melody, faint yet resonant.

10:14p.m. Three texts from Dean. Strange.

Dean: Bro, we need to talk.
Dean: Yo.
Dean: You there?

Dean hasn't ever been the type to text more than once. A sense of unease gnaws at me, a small pit settling in my stomach, signalling that something isn't quite right.

M: Sorry mate I was asleep. Everything good?

Dean reads my message immediately and begins typing. I'm now sitting upright in full anticipation.

Dean: I need to see you. Meet me at the end of Delilah's road by the alley?

M: On my way.

I rub my eyes in an attempt to wake myself up and swiftly grab my bike key as I head out. My mind is a whirlpool of thoughts once again.

I soon reach the alley and catch sight of Dean, resting against the railing with a large, black duffel bag at his feet. His face looks grey and lifeless, like some kind of zombie. He's running out of time. I remove my helmet and approach him slowly.

"You alright?" I ask with concern. He doesn't respond, instead he picks up the bag at his feet and passes it to me. A pause lingers as I grasp the bag, a silent plea for any semblance of an explanation.

"You're gonna need that." He states, breaking the silence. I crouch down eagerly and unzip the bag, revealing a handgun nestled on top of a shitload of cash. At least ten grand.

What the fuck is going on.

I glance up at him, searching his face for clues, but his expression remains inscrutable.

"They dug up a body at the tunnel today." His words send a jolt of shock through me, my mind racing to comprehend the situation. "I don't really care what happened," he continues, "All I know, is that you've gotta get out of here, and luckily for you, so do I." I stare at Dean, dumbfounded by his words. The weight of his revelation sinks in, the gravity of the situation hitting me like a ton of bricks.

"What do you mean-" I manage to mumble out as I stand back up.

"I've been dealing for a long time, and I've got myself into some serious trouble with some serious people." Dean confesses, his words heavy with the burden of truth. "If I make it out of this book bullshit alive, I'm leaving, and you're coming with me." I stop for a while to gather my thoughts.

"Leave where?" My voice cracks, the enormity of his proposal hitting me with a force that leaves me reeling.

"A little bit of everywhere," He chuckles, "We're on the run. We can't hang around anywhere for too long."

"But we have a life here."

"Neither of us will once all these fuckers figure out where we are. I'm not asking. I'm telling you, we're leaving." The bag in my hands suddenly feels like a ticket to an uncertain future, a future I never thought I'd face.

A murderer on the run with his drug dealer friend. It's like something out of a movie. A bad movie.

"I found a B&B a few hours away in the middle of nowhere that I think is a good place to start." I shake my head, hoping to shake away all of my new responsibilities along with it.

"How did you hide all of this?"

"Marcus, we've been hiding forever. Hiding from our childhood, hiding from our futures, hiding from ourselves. And after seeing those files and dealing with this fucking book, I think its time we stopped."

With a mix of fear and resignation, I nod, acknowledging the reality of the situation.

"What about Delilah?" I ask. Dean's face desaturates even further and he scratches nervously at his jaw.

"She wants to stay." He states.

"She can't stay here, she'll be a target."

"I know," He admits, his voice filled with stress and worry. "But her family is here. I can't pull her from them."

"Fuck."

"I know, man. I'm shitting myself about it. I gave her a gun and convinced her to install a load of security cameras." He pauses, "You're gonna have to do the same for Sienna."

I think the fuck not.

I laugh,

"Sienna will be coming with me, whether she likes it or not." I declare firmly, leaving no room for debate in my words.

"She'll be distraught."

"Maybe," I concede. "But she'll be safe." Dean nods slowly, understanding the weight of the responsibility we both carry.

"Are you gonna sort this book out?" He asks, desperately.

"Of course. Dean, I'm not gonna let you die." I promise, "Millie's gonna come around, I know it. I'm just waiting for her to text me." He nods his head again and briefly places his hand on my shoulder.

"As soon as it's shut, we leave. Got it?"

"Got it."

With that, Dean texts me the address of the B&B, runs me through a few of his plans and takes off back to Delilah's house. I feel the weight of his words crushing down on me, heavier than the duffel bag in my hands. The night air feels charged with uncertainty as I contemplate the sudden turn our lives have taken. How did we end up in this mess? Now alone in the alley, I lean against the cold metal railing, the dimly lit street casting elongated shadows around me. I light a cigarette, the ember casting an intermittent glow against the night, and for the first time in a long while, fear clenches at my insides. Not only are the police after me, and closing in quickly, but now Dean's secret enemies will be hot on my tail too. A bone-deep chill sets in, amplified by the swirling mist of the night. The smoke spirals up, dissipating into the inky sky, disappearing like my chances of staying here unscathed.

The duffel bag at my feet feels like an anchor, grounding me in this unexpected turmoil. A gun and cash, a testament to a life I thought I'd be able to just leave behind. Thought I'd gotten away with. But now, it's resurfaced, like all problems in my life, they creep back in; nightmares knocking on the door.

This time, I have no choice but to answer.

CHAPTER 28:

SOUR

I stumble into my bedroom, shutting the door behind me, and unceremoniously toss the bag onto the floor. Without warning, my legs give way and I can no longer stand, dropping to a crouch as the gravity of it all hits me. My vision becomes speckled and the room begins to spin. This is it. The mirror I've avoided, the reflection of the monster I've become, the monster I never wanted to face. My hands begin to tingle and I place one firmly on the floor in an attempt to steady myself.

Guilt begins to claw at my chest, a crushing weight that suffocates, a raw, searing pain that rips through my being. Killing is one sin, but tearing Sienna from her mother, thrusting her into a storm she didn't ask for is a cold, despicable evil that I'll never forgive myself for. It sears at my soul. A sob escapes me, the first crack in the fortress of indifference I'd spent my entire life carefully constructing.

I'm in an awakening, a reckoning, a gut-wrenching realisation that I've become the very nightmare I always feared. And I have no choice but to confront it head-on, to bear the burden of my actions and the inevitable fall out they bring. Each breath feels like a stab, each sob a rending of my heart. The walls I've erected around my emotions, the barriers that shielded me from the world's cruelty, crumble like sandcastles against an incoming tide. Now I am that cruelty. A fortress of indifference, now in ruins, revealing the wicked, heinous man I've become. Inhuman.

I lift the gun from the bag and hold it in my trembling, blood soaked hands. Knowing this gun can only symbolise that there is more to come. I'm forced to confront the atrocities I've committed, and I'm fine with them. I'll kill anyone. Fuck it. But now I must face the consequences of much bigger crimes that will engulf Sienna, the innocent soul I've unwittingly pulled into my darkened existence. She, my sweet angel, who already bore the scars of losing her parents, now faces the agony of separation from her adoptive mother. And it's my doing. The anguish tears through me like a hurricane, ripping apart the fabric of my being. The tears flow freely now, cascading down my cheeks in a torrent, mirroring the flood of despair and self-reproach drowning my conscience.

Although I'm painfully aware this upheaval is for her safety, there's no way she'll ever comprehend that. The thought tightens a vice around my heart. The thought of bringing my sweet back to a place of such familiar pain is a concept so sickening. How could I? How could I possibly look into those beautiful eyes, those eyes that have finally sought refuge in mine, now bound to see a tormentor instead of a protector? How do I make her understand that I've become a monster, a villain in her story, all for the sake of keeping her safe? My heart shatters at the thought of betraying the trust she'd placed in me, tarnishing the fragile sanctuary I'd worked to build for her.

I yearn for absolution, a sliver of hope in this abyss I've descended into. But the truth remains; the monster within me is the monster Sienna now faces, and I'm powerless to change that reality.

I'll make things right for her. One day. It's a promise I make to myself, and I don't break promises. Ever. I'll kill every fucker on this planet to fulfill my promise if that's what it takes. I'll slit every throat. She *will* have a good life. I will change things for her. I'll make sure of it. I've made my peace with the atrocities I've committed, but for Sienna, I'll fight tooth and nail to ensure her innocence remains untouched.

My sweet's innocence is my responsibility; her happiness and safety too. And I'll do what's necessary to ensure her sanctuary, even if it means embracing the shadows once more, or a thousand times more. The thought of sacrificing everything to protect her, including my own humanity, sears through me.

Fucking pull yourself together, Marcus.

With a firm resolve and one large sharp breath, the emotional turmoil dissipates, replaced by an eerie cruelness. The fortress of indifference begins to rebuild, layer by layer, obscuring the fractures of empathy that briefly cracked its surface. I stand, the room still spinning but my mind resolute. The vulnerability, the anguish, I shove them deep into the recesses of my being, locking them away. The monster reclaims its dominion, a cold, calculated protector emerging once again.

The tears that had once cascaded freely, now a distant memory as I wipe away the remnants of any weakness. The reflection in that mirror morphs from that of a tormented soul to a steely-eyed harbinger of my own salvation, and Sienna's. I crack my neck and square my shoulders, as a smirk grows on my lips. The familiar chill seeping back into my veins, numbing the raw ache within. I'm back.

Alone in the stillness of my room, I raise the gun, its weight a sinister reassurance in my grip. I don't flinch. Instead, I embrace the chilling certainty that I am no longer the man I once pretended to be. The gun, an extension of my will, whispers promises of power, of control over a world that dared to challenge me for my entire life. My finger hovers over the trigger, a moment frozen in time, where the past and the present collide in a fucked up embrace. The man I was fades into obscurity, a figment of a distant memory. I've willingly surrendered to the allure of this newfound malevolence.

In this room, where the air hangs heavy with my decisions, I make peace with the monster I've become. I embrace him. I am the architect of my own damnation, a maestro orchestrating the symphony of my own malevolent destiny. The monster within is no longer a foe to be fought; it's a companion I've chosen to accept, a relentless shadow that cloaks me in its perverse clutch. The gun doesn't shake in my hand. Instead, it becomes an instrument of my will, a tool to carve out my new path.

Suddenly, a vibration in my pocket jolts me out of the trance-like state I'd sunk into. Finally, the text from an unknown number I've been waiting for.

Unknown: It's Millie. I'm going to close the book, for Dean. I'll be at Orchid's ASAP. Don't make me wait.

The room feels foreign, almost surreal, as I stand in its midst, surrounded by the fragments of a life I'm about to abandon. The black duffel bag, my new faithful companion, lays open, its yawning mouth waiting to swallow the remnants of my existence. Each item I pack, the clothes hastily folded, the stacks of cash neatly aligned, and the gun cold and unforgiving, feels like a shard of the life I'm leaving behind. There's an unsettling finality to the act of packing, as if each piece I place within the confines of the bag seals a chapter of my life. The book resting on top, the source of all of this bullshit.

The sense of unreality thickens the air around me. Here I am, leaving behind the familiar, a semblance of normalcy; all for a world of uncertainty, a life of crime. It's a dizzying juxtaposition. As I zip the bag shut, the sound echoes with a hollow finality, a closure to the life that Skylar's family had offered me. My heart pounds against the cage of my chest, a cacophony of emotions. A tinge of remorse for the life I'm willingly discarding. Each fold of fabric, each touch of the gun's steel against my palm; these actions carry a weight that transcends the physical.

I pause, taking a final sweeping glance around the room, trying to imprint every detail into my memory. Procrastinating my departure from the familiar. I almost feel a little ungrateful. Staring down at my new makeshift bed that Skylar's father had put up for me. With a deep breath that quivers in my chest, I sling the bag over my shoulder. The strap digs deep into my skin, a constant reminder that within its confines lies not just my belongings, but the fragments of a past life I've willingly surrendered.

As I walk, the hallway seems to warp, the walls closing in on me, suffocatingly close yet infinitely distant. My mind teeters on the edge of acceptance and denial, wavering between the surrealness of this departure and the undeniable truth that I've chosen this path willingly. Leaving behind a home, a life, a family. All the things I spent my entire childhood longing for. They're at my fingertips and I'm pulling away.

But if it means Sienna will be safe, and mine, I'll give up anything.

I make my way to Skylar's room and knock on the door, tapping a message into the group chat amidst the anticipation of Sky's response. She opens the door and is less than pleased to see me.

"What the fuck do you want?" she snaps.

Chapter 28

"We're closing the book. Right now." Skylar's eyes narrow, suspicion laced with excitement.

"For real?" She asks

"Yeah, for real," I reply, my voice carrying the weight of determination and urgency. "It's time."

"Oh my god." She flusters, grabbing her phone from her bed. "Okay, okay," Skylar mutters nervously, "Let's do this."

"I need you to get a car." I instruct.

"A car?"

"Yes. If this doesn't work we're gonna need to get him to the hospital." She nods, the urgency in my voice resonating with her innate understanding of our covert world.

"Got it. I'll be as quick as I can."

CHAPTER 29:
LOCK FIX

I bolt out of the house, urgency propelling me as I rush towards Orchid's. With no time for a helmet, I race through the streets, my hair whipping in the wind. The roads become a blur, the city lights streaking past as if in a hurry to escape the night. The urgency of our situation eclipses all other concerns. The roar of passing cars, the blaring horns; they all fade into insignificance against the gravity of what we're about to undertake. I weave through the traffic, my movements fluid and calculated, each turn a well-practised manoeuvre honed by necessity. The roads, once familiar, now seem like an obstacle course, every bend a hurdle to overcome in this race against time. My mind races faster than my bike, a cacophony of thoughts urging me forward. Every passing second feels like an eternity, the moments stretching and compressing in an erratic dance with my pounding heartbeats.

The screech of my bike as I skid into the car park punctuates the silent tension of the group, who are standing tensely in a circle. Dean barely keeping himself standing. Adrenaline courses through me as I leap off the bike, urgency propelling my every movement. Millie, standing at a cautious distance from the others, casts a wary glance in my direction, a silent acknowledgment laden with uncertainty. The air hangs heavy with anticipation, the collective tension notable as I head join the circle, their faces etched with a mix of apprehension and resolve. I throw the bag to the floor and pull out the book with purpose. I lock eyes with Millie, a silent nod between us affirming our shared resolve. She walks timidly towards me and grabs the other half of the book.

Millie and I stand opposite one another, gripping the book tight, our gazes pinned onto the stubborn lock. As our fingers edge closer, a subtle resistance emerges, a minuscule defiance that echoes the colossal power imprisoned within the pages. It's as though the lock itself hesitates, whispering reminders of the untamed forces. I push Millie on with my determined gaze, forcing her to mirror me. With a shared glance that speaks volumes, we lean forward, fingers hovering over the lock. It resists, fighting against our unified effort, a silent protest against the impending culmination of this journey. But we persist, applying as much pressure as we can. It begins to progress and I feel the closure beneath my fingertips looming closer.

The resistance intensifies, the lock pushing back against our insistence. Each push, each attempt to snap it shut feels like a battle against an unyielding force. But with an unspoken pact, a fusion of resolve, we push harder, gritting our teeth against the resistance, our knuckles turning white with exertion. The others stand around with faces of hope and pleading. The lock begrudgingly begins to relent, its rigid defiance giving way to the persistent pressure we apply.

The moment of truth dawns upon us, a crescendo in the symphony of our combined efforts. With one final surge of resilient determination, the lock yields. It clicks into place with a resounding finality, as if acquiescing to the force of our collective resolve.

An abrupt explosion of radiant light erupts from the book, a coruscating beam that pierces the night sky, illuminating the world in a breathtaking display of otherworldly splendour. The air crackles with raw, unrestrained magic, an ethereal shockwave reverberating outward from the epicentre of our unified action. The luminous cascade engulfs us, bathing the surroundings in an incandescent glow that dances and weaves through the night. The sheer brilliance blinds our senses momentarily, yet we remain holding the book tight, permitting the magical light show to play around us.

All of a sudden, a thunderous, resonating boom echoes across the vast expanse of the car park, a deep and sonorous sound that seems to reverberate through the very fabric of existence. Far more intense than the first explosion we had felt. The ground quivers beneath our feet, an imperceptible tremor echoing the magnitude of the magical release. It's a sound that seems to carry the weight of a thousand destinies shifting, a testament to the monumental shift occurring in this space. Amidst the cacophony of sound and light, our senses momentarily overwhelmed, a profound sense of fulfilment washes over us.

I turn my head to face Dean who has his eyes tightly shut, with Delilah held tightly in his arms. Tears of relief and desperation streaming down her face, glistening in the brilliant radiance that envelops the air. It's a moment that transcends the mundane, an extraordinary convergence of forces that binds our fates together.

Time seems to stretch and fold in on itself, a poignant pause in the midst of the chaos that had unfurled in our lives. As the iridescent glow slowly recedes, casting a serene blanket over the car park, the edges of my vision clear. The thrum of magic that had enveloped us begins to ebb, leaving behind a sense of serenity and fulfilment.

The radiance dims, revealing Dean's face fully. His once pallid complexion slowly breathes with life, each inhalation filling his lungs with newfound strength. I observe, a quiet spectator in this surreal moment, as Dean's eyelids flutter open. His irises glisten with a rekindled light, carrying the weight of emotions known only to those who've tiptoed along the precipice of loss. Delilah remains cradled in his arms, her teary gaze meeting his, an unspoken conversation passing between them. It's a shared relief, a silent understanding of the edge they nearly slipped from.

A soft smile graces Dean's lips, a gentle acknowledgment of the tumultuous journey they've just weathered. The weight lifts off my chest, replaced by a swell of relief. It's as though fate rewound its threads, granting him a second chance, one we have fought relentlessly to secure. Delilah's eyes shimmer with tears, a testament to the cascade of emotions surging within her. Joy, relief, and a profound love intermingle, weaving an intricate tapestry of emotions. Her fingers tighten around Dean, anchoring herself in the reality of his living, breathing presence.

My gaze shifts across the group, noting the shared sense of accomplishment etched into their expressions. Millie stands beside me, her shoulders easing, the tension of the moment dissipating. The car park holds witness to an otherworldly tableau; a victory shining amidst the mundane backdrop of concrete. Dean's eyes find mine as he keeps Delilah held tight, a silent bridge forming between us. Gratitude shimmers in his gaze, an unspoken depth that transcends words. His lips part, a silent 'thank you,' though no sound carries in the serene aftermath of the magical burst. Yet, in that wordless exchange, our mutual understanding resonates. A smile tugs at my lips, mirroring the shared triumph binding us. It's a smile speaking volumes, a testament to the unbreakable bonds in this circle.

My family.

I turn to face my beautiful little Sienna, her face drowned in unconcealable happiness. I drop the book to the floor and charge to her, lifting her effortlessly into my arms, her legs wrapping instinctively around me. Her sweet scent breaks into my nostrils as I bury my face into her neck. My hand firmly gripping her hair in a celebratory embrace. As she giggles and squirms in my arms, her joy reverberates through me. It's an unadulterated happiness, a feeling so pure that it momentarily erases the weight of the trials we've weathered. Her laughter dances on the edges of the car park, a triumphant melody. The vibrant spectrum of emotions spreads like wildfire, engulfing us all in a radiant moment of unfiltered elation. It's the melody of victory serenading us, painting the night with hues of hope, relief, and unabashed happiness. I cherish this instant, embracing Sienna like she's the very embodiment of the world's newfound harmony.

Soon enough the others pile onto our embrace. Enfolding us all in a warm, collective squeeze. Arms wrap around shoulders, and bodies meld together in a cascade of emotions; a symphony of relief, joy, and undiluted love. We tighten and tighten together, as if trying to etch this monumental moment into our memories forever. As the embrace gradually loosens, the shared sense of camaraderie lingers in the air like a gentle breeze. It's the kind of unity that cements bonds and fortifies spirits.

A reminder that amidst the chaos, we stand united, a family forged not by blood, but by the trials we've endured together.

CHAPTER 30:
TIME TO GO

As the group disentangles from the embrace, a shadow falls over our collective joy. Millie stands apart, her silhouette etched in seclusion, her face etched in a tapestry of bitterness and betrayal. The accusatory silence she exudes cuts through the elation, leaving a disquieting hush in its wake. Sensing the sudden shift, I glance around, and the tendrils of unease tighten within me. Millie, the linchpin of our journey, now appears distant, alienated amidst our celebration. She stands, a lone sentinel of resentment amidst our jubilant tableau. Her eyes bore into us with a mix of anger and hurt, her for-once-warm demeanour cloaked in the frigid chill of betrayal.

We stand almost in a line against her, as if we're ready for some kind of battle.

"So that's it?" She starts, "Now that you got what you wanted from me, I'm thrown to the side?" We look at one another in complete confusion. All beyond fed up with her negative attitude.

"What are you talking about?" Birdie snaps back.

Fire vs Fire.

"You think we pre-scheduled our group hug or something? Just join in if you want to, don't try to make this about you, Millie."

"Shut up Birdie! None of this would have happened without me. Where's my credit? Huh?" She squeals like a lunatic.

"You're a psycho." Birdie continues. The air crackles with emotions as Millie's frustration ignites like a wildfire, engulfing the fragile peace we had just tasted. Birdie's retort, fueled by the same intensity, only adds fuel to the fire, a clash of wills in a moment of escalating turmoil.

"Alright, alright. Enough, both of you." Dean interrupts in an attempt to bring back the celebratory atmosphere.

But the flames of conflict are already ablaze.

"You can't just blow up on us, Millie!" Delilah's voice quivers, her eyes brimming with unshed tears, a reflection of the hurt and confusion that has unexpectedly swept through our group. Sienna grips my hand tightly, her wide eyes darting between each person in the tense standoff. She hates conflict, my innocent angel.

"Stop it, please!" Her voice, small yet filled with genuine distress, cuts through the escalating argument. Her plea seems to echo in the car park, a poignant reminder of the ripple effects of our discord. I envelop her in a tight embrace and gently guide her towards my bag, hoping to divert her attention from the escalating argument.

I zip up the bag and sling it over my shoulder once again, Sienna's gaze suddenly filled with concern.

"What was that in your bag?"

Uh oh.

"Don't worry about it, sweet-"

"Was that a gun?" She asks, her eyes widening. Her voice trembles with a mix of alarm and uncertainty. The innocent honesty in her question feels like a sharp pin prick against my knowledge of what happens next.

"It's nothing, okay? I'll explain later. I promise"

The situation's escalating gravity sets in as Sienna's grip tightens around my hand. Her eyes, wide with a mix of fear and confusion, search for reassurance in my gaze. My attention snaps back to the group, the turmoil between Birdie and Millie still flaring. Their heated exchange seems to have reached a point of no return, caught in a vicious cycle of accusations and frustration.

Suddenly, an unsettling chill courses through me as, through the argument, I hear the faint sound of sirens in the distance. Am I paranoid? Maybe. But where else are they going in this small residential area at this time? I look to Dean and attempt to draw his attention to the distant echo of sirens.

The sirens, faint at first, now grow louder, punctuating the silence like an ominous drumbeat.

My heart races, the adrenaline-fueled urgency heightening my senses. Dean, his eyes mirroring my concern, nods in silent acknowledgment. There's no need for further explanation; the threat of the approaching sirens speaks volumes. I turn my attention back to her, crouching to meet her gaze, trying to paint a reassuring smile on my face despite the unrest brewing within.

"Sweet, we have to go." I tell her softly.

"Go where?"

"You just have to trust me."

"Marcus, I don't understand." Her eyes now frantically scanning my face for answers. The sirens grow louder and louder and I feel the clock ticking against me. I begin to feel my heartbeat take over my entire body.

The dissonance of sirens swells like a relentless symphony in my mind, each wail slicing through my brain and ringing in my ears. What was once a distant echo now feels like an ominous, impending doom, closing in with a relentless intensity. Every nerve in my body tingles with an urgent alarm, the growing intensity of the sirens reverberating through the very core of my being. My thoughts scramble, a rush of disjointed fragments that struggle to form a coherent plan amidst this noise. Each siren feels like a countdown, a merciless metronome ticking away the moments we have left before something cataclysmic unfolds.

"Sweet, please. Get on the bike." I plead.

"You have to tell me what's going on."

"I'm not gonna ask you again. Get on the bike or I'm putting you on it myself. Please, sweet. Please. For once in your life stop fighting me." She stands still, staring through my eyes, longing for an explanation I don't have time to give. With no more time to waste, I scoop Sienna into my arms, her small frame fitting perfectly against my chest.

"Fuck off, Millie. Nobody gives a shit! You're nothing but a pretentious bully!" Birdie shouts in the background. I glance over briefly to catch sight of Millie turning and beginning to walk away.

"I love you, sweet. I'm doing this for you. Everything is for you, my angel." I whisper to Sienna, the urgency in my voice unmissable. Without listening for a response, I sprint toward the bike, my heart pounding in rhythm with the blaring sirens that have still continued to grow impossibly louder. I sit her on the bike, placing a reassuring kiss on her forehead before mounting on infront of her.

"Hold on to me tight, sweet." Her tiny arms grip tight around my waist and I rev the engine. The tense atmosphere around us feels charged with impending chaos, the sirens now roaring with an alarming proximity. My focus narrows solely on Sienna's safety, an urgency that eclipses everything else.

A sudden intrusion sends shockwaves through the air, disrupting the charged atmosphere of tension and escalating emotions. It happens in the blink of an eye; a car swerves into the car park. An ear-splitting screech of tires pierces the air, followed by an ominous thud that plunges us into a sudden, eerie silence. Dust and dirt erupt in a frenzied whirlwind, enveloping the immediate space in a shroud of debris. The sound of the collision lingers. A tense stillness blankets the car park, an unexpected interlude. Dust motes hang suspended in the air, caught in the fading echoes of the abrupt impact.

The cloud of debris eventually disperses, unveiling the scene beneath its transient veil. A haunting sight comes into view in the form of Millie lying motionless on the ground.

"Oh my God." Sienna whispers behind me. I instinctively shield Sienna's view, my fingers tightening around her hand in an effort to shield her from the distressing sight.

"Don't look, sweet. turn around." I order, in all attempts to protect her innocence from the jarring scene in front of us. The car, an ominous harbinger of catastrophe, stands sentinel in the midst of the chaos, a chilling reminder of the unforeseen. Its metal frame, now an instrument of terror. Dean, his once-confident demeanour now stripped bare, steps forward hesitantly, his eyes fixated on the motionless figure.

"Is she... is she alive?" His voice, a mere whisper.

Time slows down momentarily and suddenly blue lights from a trailing police car fill the car park in front of me. The light spills across the dirt, a sinister glow outlining the unmoving silhouette of Millie on the ground. The flashes illuminate the significant puddle of blood now pooling on the floor around her head. The life knocked out of her entirely. She lies dead. But I've seen much worse now. My mind briefly flickers back to the image of

Skinny Jeans' blood trickling down my arm. I have to get used to death. To murder. After all, it seems I'm going to be doing a lot more of it.

I turn to make sure Sienna isn't looking and tighten my grip on her hand, rubbing my thumb back and forth in a soothing motion. We have to get out of here. I rev my bike again and scan the escape gaps in the crime scene now settling in front of me.

"Skylar?" Birdie's voice suddenly wavers, with a mix of disbelief and dread. Her abrupt exclamation shatters the eerie silence that envelops us, her hands instinctively rising to cover her gaping mouth. I turn to her, the confusion etched across my face. Following her gaze, my eyes fall upon the killer-car, now a haunting monument to the chaos that has unfurled. There, behind the wheel, sits Skylar. Her eyes wide with shock, a visage of terror etched across her face as though she's trapped in a nightmare from which she cannot wake.

A sinister smirk, filled with satisfaction, takes over my lips.

Well, Sky… *I guess that makes two of us.*

'Saving Sweet Sienna'

Publishing 2024

Playlist

Chapter 1:
Sleepwalker - Akiaura, LONOWN, STM

Chapter 2:
Drowning - Vague003, Sadistik

Chapter 3:
Your face - Wisp

Chapter 4:
What the hell - Avril Lavigne

Chapter 5:
Wait - M83

Chapter 6:
FASHION (Slow) - Britney Manson

Chapter 7:
Aglow - The Rare Occasions

Chapter 8:
Haunt me (x3) - Teen Suicide

Chapter 9:
Mountains - Message To Bears

Chapter 10:
Memory Reboot - VØJ, Narvent

Nothing's Gonna Hurt You Baby - Cigarettes After Sex

Chapter 21 :
Fluxxwave (Slowed + Reverb) - Clovis Reyes

LOVELY BASTARDS - ZWEIHVNDXR

Chapter 22 :
Roslyn - Ben Pellow

Chapter 23 :
Death Is No More - BLESSED MANE

Chapter 24 :
505 - Arctic Monkeys

Weightless - Chiiild

Chapter 25 :
Resonance - Home

1979 (Remastered 2012) - The Smashing Pumpkins

Chapter 26 :
Need 2 - Pinegrove

Me and You - Cold Hart, LiL Peep

Chapter 27 :
Into Me - Glare

Chapter 28 :
You're Somebody Else - Flora cash

Toxic City - LiL Peep

Chapter 29 :
Acid Rain - Lorn

Chapter 30 :
untitled #13 - glwzbll

ABOUT THE AUTHOR

Amber Fawn, born 2002, is an indie author, specialising in Romance & Dark romance. Her passion for reading and writing began as early as 3 years old when she forced herself to learn how to read. Her preferred writing style is often on the darker side, experimenting with elements of gore and psychological trauma.

Website: amberfawnauthor.com

Instagram: @amberfawnauthor